STERNER STUFF

Who would want to kill a harmless priest in the quiet Cotswold market town of Colombury? Surprisingly, it transpires that there is a wide choice of suspects, including, amongst others, a brigadier who has quarrelled with the priest, a vagrant whom he had befriended, and the thief who stole a historic chalice from the church.

The police are able to establish that the killing took place within a narrow time frame, but they are less successful in persuading witnesses to come forward. Though it is believed that a nurse from the nearby hospital was in the church around the time of the murder, she seems unwilling to help the police with their inquiries. With the discovery of a second body, fear stalks the community. Could there be yet a third murder?

Detective Superintendent Tansey faces a difficult task as he tries to untangle the relationships between the various individuals involved and, as usual, John Penn provides a fascinating plot with many twists and surprises in which police procedure and character are inextricably mixed, with unexpected and bizarre results.

STERNER STUFF

John Penn

HarperCollins*Publishers*

This book is fiction. Any relationship between the characters in this novel and any person who exists in reality is purely coincidental.

Collins Crime
An imprint of HarperCollins*Publishers*
77–85 Fulham Palace Road, London W6 8JB

First published in Great Britain
in 1997 by Collins Crime

1 3 5 7 9 10 8 6 4 2

A catalogue record for this book is
available from the British Library

ISBN 0 00 232634 5

Set in Meridien and Bodoni

Typeset by Rowland Phototypesetting Ltd
Bury St Edmunds, Suffolk
Printed and bound in Great Britain by
Caledonian International Book Manufacturing Ltd, Glasgow

'Ambition should be made of sterner stuff.'
Julius Caesar

CHAPTER 1

The priest raised his head abruptly as the door of the sacristy creaked open. There had been no knock. A little stiffly, because he had been praying for some time, he rose from the prie-dieu and turned to face his visitor.

Ten years ago, when he had first come to the Cotswold market town of Colombury as parish priest to the Roman Catholic church of St Stephen, he had brought an old prie-dieu into the sacristy and, if the opportunity arose, before putting on his sacerdotal robes, he liked to pray for a while to clear his mind and calm his spirit before going into the church to say the Saturday evening Mass. But he didn't object to being interrupted. He always left the door of the sacristy ajar and, if any of his parishioners wished to seek him out and have a private word with him, they were welcome. If the door was shut it was accepted that someone was already with him, and it was necessary to wait or to go away. This custom was known to all his parishioners, and was not abused. But few would have entered the sacristy without knocking, and the priest was not surprised by the identity of the newcomer. 'Ah, it's you,' he said. 'I've been thinking of you and I was half expecting you. I knew you would come to see me, sooner or later.'

There was no response and the priest became aware that his heart was beating very fast, though not from fear. He was not afraid of physical violence, not until he saw the knife, and then there was only a split second in which to realize that he was about to be killed. He flung up an arm to defend himself, but he was much too slow. The blow was precise and he died instantly.

*   *   *

With great care the killer drew the knife out of the body and wiped it on the priest's soutane. He took off the gloves he had been wearing and produced a plastic shopping bag from his pocket – he had already lined it with newspapers. He put the knife and the gloves in the bag. He inspected the front of the light raincoat he was wearing and, as he had expected, found no blood on it. A careful and quick knife blow which killed immediately should produce very little blood.

Once he was free of the church he would be safe. There was no generally known connection between him and the priest that would implicate him in the killing.

He threw one last glance around the sacristy and his eye lighted upon a chalice waiting ready on a side table for the Mass that was to be at six that evening. He picked it up in his handkerchief and added it to the shopping bag; its disappearance might help to confuse the police. Then he looked at his watch. It was time to go. Surprisingly he hadn't been in the sacristy for more than two or three minutes, but someone might come into the church at any moment, and he must not be seen leaving.

He opened the door of the sacristy cautiously. The church was still in darkness except for two flickering banks of candles, one on each side, before the statues of Our Lady and St Stephen, and the meagre light they gave didn't reach the back of the building. He edged round the door and shut it behind him. Now, collar turned up and head buried in a scarf, he was no more than a deep shadow as he started quickly down the aisle.

But he was brought to an abrupt halt. Someone had uttered what sounded like a loud snore and, peering through the gloom, he saw quite close to him the outline of a man lying full length in a pew. How long had he been there? Had he seen him enter the sacristy? No, the killer reassured himself. The man – and he could guess who it was – was fast asleep, and he had kept his face well protected both entering and leaving the sacristy. Confident again, he hurried on, not pausing in his stride until, moments later, he was out of the church and walking briskly down the street.

*   *   *

As was usual, the Misses Blair – two elderly ladies in their late seventies – were the first members of the congregation to arrive for the Saturday evening Mass. Sometimes, as tonight, they were ludicrously early. They lived in Little Chipping, one of the outlying villages which was served by the priests at St Stephen's, and this was the nearest church of their faith. Although they frequently drove into Colombury, they never seemed able to calculate the time and never failed to be the first arrivals.

Nevertheless, they were surprised to find the church illuminated only by candlelight. They stood, huddled together, wondering if they had missed some announcement the previous week and had come at the wrong time. The arrival of Brigadier Wessex dispelled their doubt, although as Miss Jean, the elder of the sisters, was to tell Detective Superintendent Tansey later, the brigadier seemed 'rather fraught'.

'You stay where you are, ladies, and I'll turn the lights on,' he commanded. 'Father must have been delayed, and we are very early, aren't we?' He laughed as if he had made a joke. 'I won't be a moment.'

In fact, fumbling in the semi-darkness, the brigadier took a few minutes before he found the switches and turned on the lights. He was immediately aware of three facts. The church door was sighing closed as if someone had just departed, for obviously no one had followed him in. The Blair sisters had not waited as he had suggested, but had felt their way up the aisle and had reached their customary pew on the right-hand side. The third fact that blew the other two from his mind was that Alfred Yorke had returned.

He had hoped to have seen the back of Yorke, who hadn't been around for the past two or three weeks, but here he was again, the epitome of everything that the brigadier despised, because Alfred Yorke was a wastrel. Innumerable attempts had been made to help him, to find him a home and work, to restore his self-respect, but they had had no effect. He had resisted them all.

Yorke preferred to remain unshaven and unwashed, to wear filthy clothes, to live off benefits and what he could cadge from charitable individuals, to sleep rough in fine weather, and when the weather was bad to break into garden sheds and outhouses or, what was infinitely worse in Brigadier Wessex's opinion, to spend the night in the church. It didn't worry the man that he was locked in and, before he had been caught, he had slept throughout a snowy period the previous winter in the doubtful comfort of a confessional.

He treated St Stephen's as his home and, when apprehended by the police for petty crimes, always gave it as his address. Seemingly a devout Catholic – he was a regular communicant – he didn't care if people avoided sitting near him because he smelt. He was happy to be alone and didn't appear to need companionship. Besides, if no one sat near him there was more room in the pew to spread out his sandwiches or whatever else he had found to eat.

It was this use or misuse of the church that really infuriated the brigadier. Basically John Wessex was a kind character. He would gladly have given Yorke clothes or money or food – and the best of advice – but he could not endure the ne'er-do-well's behaviour, which he considered to be an affront to the Church of Rome and the members of St Stephen's parish in particular. His intolerance was exacerbated, though he wouldn't have admitted it, by his suspicion that Alfred Yorke, in spite of all appearances to the contrary, was in reality not a bum, but a well-educated man with a respectable background.

Recently Yorke and his behaviour had become an obsession with the brigadier, but he knew that nothing could be done as long as Father Le Merle talked about everyone being welcome in the House of God. Presumably the naïve priest had never heard of Christ driving out the money-changers.

The brigadier, who had sat down in a pew near the door, squared his already square shoulders as he watched a trickle of parishioners arriving for the Mass. No, he didn't regret what he had done. Action had been necessary. The priest was a good man, but like so many such men he was misguided, an easy dupe for creatures like Yorke.

'Brigadier!'

'Hello, what is it?'

He smiled at the tall, thin, narrow-shouldered man who was addressing him. He liked Patrick Gough. He knew that Gough's great ambition in life was to become a priest, but an ailing mother for whom he cared made this impossible at present, and Gough had settled for being a deacon. He was usually calm and quiet, but now he was visibly perturbed.

'Brigadier, I'm afraid Father Le Merle may have been taken ill. He's in the sacristy, because you can see the light under the door and I don't think he'd have gone away and left it on, the cost of electricity being what it is.' Gough was speaking very rapidly. 'But the candles on the altar aren't lit. Nothing's ready for Mass.'

'Did you knock on the sacristy door?' Wessex asked sensibly.

'Only a light tap. You know he doesn't like to be interrupted if the door's shut, because it means that someone is with him. But there was no answer – and look at the time!'

'Yes. It's getting on. I should be on my way.'

'You're not staying for Mass?' Gough was surprised.

'No, I just looked in to have a word with Father Le Merle. I'm due to meet my wife, Deirdre, at a party, and it'll take me some while to get there.'

'But you'll come with me to the sacristy first, won't you?'

The brigadier hesitated. He had no wish to go to the sacristy, but Gough's request was almost a plea; he was in some respects a timid young man and clearly he wanted support. It was difficult to refuse.

'All right, but let's be quick.'

As they hurried up the aisle, Wessex added, 'Incidentally, when I arrived this evening on the heels of the Misses Blair, the church was in darkness. It was I who turned on the lights.'

Gough, his anxiety increasing, quickened his step. 'Father always turns them on in good time,' he said.

As they passed the pew in which Alfred Yorke sprawled,

11

Gough wrinkled his nose at the too human smell. Yorke had by now finished his sandwich and had started on an apple. But Brigadier Wessex glared at the man and thought with satisfaction that, thanks to what he had done, the wastrel, deprived of Father Le Merle's support, wouldn't be despoiling the church for much longer.

They reached the sacristy and the brigadier motioned Gough ahead. Reluctantly the deacon knocked on the door and, when there was no answer, knocked again, more loudly.

'Open it, man,' Wessex said impatiently. 'Go on!'

With a questioning shrug, Gough did as he was told, his lips already framing an apology for interrupting the priest. But no words came. Instead, he drew a sharp breath and involuntarily stepped back as he saw Father Le Merle lying on the floor in a small pool of blood. It was not a pretty sight and he felt the vomit rise in his throat.

'Oh God!' he moaned. 'Oh God! Poor Father!'

The brigadier thrust him aside. The sight of blood didn't worry him; in a distinguished army career he had seen many more horrifying scenes than the one that confronted him now, and he was accustomed to death. He bent and felt for a pulse in the priest's throat, at the same time making a quick appraisal of the situation. It was a perfunctory gesture. Father Le Merle was obviously dead.

'Shall I fetch a – a doctor?' Gough asked doubtfully.

'No point,' John Wessex replied. 'But I'm afraid we'll have to send for the police. You'd better go across to the presbytery. I shall never understand why they can't have a phone in the church.'

It was impossible to hide the fact that something was wrong. Patrick Gough, his face white and strained, was striding down the aisle as fast as his long legs would take him, and his urgency communicated itself to those sitting in the pews nearest to him. Their anxiety spread like the rustle of leaves until it seemed to John Wessex as if everyone were staring at him as he stood in front of the sacristy door, as if on guard.

12

A regular attendant at the six o'clock Saturday Mass, who also happened to be Wessex's bank manager, got up from his seat and came forward to him. 'Is there trouble, Brigadier? It's very late. Mass should have begun ages ago.'

Wessex made up his mind. Once Sergeant Donaldson, who was in charge of the Colombury police station, arrived and realized that he was dealing with a murder, he would insist that everything should be done by the book. Donaldson was a punctilious little so-and-so, and was capable of keeping the entire congregation in their places until he had first satisfied himself of the need, and then summoned help from his head-quarters, the Thames Valley Police Force in Kidlington, out-side Oxford. They could all be there till midnight or after, which was utterly unnecessary.

'I'm about to make an announcement,' he said.

He went and stood at the lectern, where he felt at home because he often read the lesson from there. 'Ladies and gentlemen,' he began formally, as if he were addressing a board meeting, 'I regret to tell you that there will be no Mass here this evening. Father Le Merle has had – had a – a serious accident in the sacristy. I can tell you no more at present. Mr Gough has gone to fetch the authorities, and there seems no good reason why you should all stay. I think it best if everyone left the church and went home. Thank you.'

There was a general murmur of concern for Father Le Merle, but people obediently gathered up their belongings and shuffled to their feet. It didn't seem to occur to anyone to question John Wessex's instructions. After all, the briga-dier was a man of standing in the community, a magistrate, a governor of the hospital and the local school and a long-time member of the church council. Moreover, as was to be expected, in spite of one slight falter he had spoken with authority.

The reason for the falter was Alfred Yorke, or rather his absence. As the brigadier made his little speech he had been looking to see the reactions of his audience, and his eye had lighted on the pew where Yorke had been sitting. There were the sandwich wrapping and the apple core, but Yorke himself had vanished.

There was little time to consider the matter, however. Although the brigadier had said he could tell them no more, he could not avoid being besieged by questions as people started to leave the church. How bad was Father Le Merle? What had happened? Could they help? Had Father Hanson been told? (Father Hanson was the assistant priest.) Had Mr Gough gone to the presbytery? Was the doctor coming? Was Father Le Merle still in the sacristy? Dealing with them as best he could, Wessex was thankful when the church had emptied.

As the door shut on the last stragglers, the deacon, Patrick Gough, reappeared. The brigadier looked at his watch. He hadn't realized how time had flown. By now the Crosses' party would be getting under way, and when he didn't appear Deirdre would worry that something had happened to him. He should have asked Gough to phone her. There was no chance now. The police would arrive at any minute.

Gough confirmed this. 'Sergeant Donaldson will be here very soon, and meanwhile he says we're not to touch any-thing. He clearly thinks we're morons. And he wasn't best pleased with your suggestion, Brigadier, that he should con-tact the Thames Valley Police headquarters at once. He said that was for him to decide.'

The brigadier sighed. 'I suppose it wasn't very tactful of me, seeing that Donaldson's such a touchy beggar, and half an hour isn't going to make much difference. What about Father Hanson and the housekeeper, Mrs . . .'

'Mrs Faudin. She wasn't there. She'd gone to visit her sister.' Gough hesitated. 'I told Father Hanson. He – he opened the door to me. He said he'd just got in and wasn't very well.'

The brigadier, like all people who are rarely ill, was impatient. 'Not very well? At a time like this? How did he look?'

'He looked pretty dreadful and –'

'What is it? Isn't he coming?'

'Yes, he's coming, but – I don't like to say this, Brigadier, but Father Hanson has been drinking, and he's far from sober.'

'Dear God!' exclaimed John Wessex. It was not often that he blasphemed.

CHAPTER 2

Angela Cross prided herself on being a good hostess and she knew instinctively that the party was not going as she would wish, but she couldn't fathom the reason. A tall Brünnhilde of a woman with natural copper-coloured hair, she looked around her drawing room as if to seek an explanation. She caught her husband's eye and smiled.

Bernard Cross topped his wife by half an inch, but there were those who claimed that when it came to drive and personality she far outstripped him, and that much of the success in his career was due to her. They were wrong. Although he valued her support and, over the years, had come to rely on it, it had never been essential to him. He was an intelligent, capable man, who had made a success of both his marriage and his career. He was, at this time, the manager of the Colombury General Hospital Trust, a demanding and well-paid job.

He returned his Angela's smile and gave an almost imperceptible shrug. He sensed her unease. They had planned this party well in advance and with great care. It was to be a welcome, probably one of several, that would be offered to Lance Ritchie, newly appointed gynaecological consultant to the hospital, and his wife, Rhoda. But it was not to be an entirely medical in-house occasion.

On the contrary, it was to be a small party, drinks followed by a buffet supper, which would be less formal than dinner, and the guests had been chosen with consideration to give the Ritchies a chance to meet some local people outside the profession. The Crosses lived in a large house on the outskirts of Colombury, and they were mainly entertaining their neighbours, who with only one or two exceptions had no connection with the hospital. The exceptions, not counting wives, were Brigadier Wessex, who was a governor of the Trust and Dr Alan Porter, the police surgeon.

Why the party hadn't 'jelled' was what was puzzling Angela Cross. It was true that the Ritchies had arrived rather late and both appeared to be anxious and worried; she wondered if they had had a row before setting out, but that was not her business. She thought that, as the party was being given for them, they should make some effort, but they did not seem to agree. Lance Ritchie, tall and absurdly good-looking, was not hiding the fact that his thoughts were elsewhere; Lorna Porter, who was talking to him, threw Angela an agonized glance, asking for help. Rhoda Ritchie seemed equally at odds with the group she was with, saying in a loud voice that she couldn't understand what people found to do in the Cotswolds, but then she was a Londoner. At this rate, their hostess thought grimly, the Ritchies were not likely to be popular in the district.

Going to rescue Lorna Porter from Ritchie, Angela was waylaid by Deirdre Wessex. 'My dear, I'm so worried about John. I can't think what's happened to him. He should have been here before me but he still hasn't arrived. Perhaps he's had an accident.'

'I expect he's just been held up somewhere.' Eager to reach her objective, Angela produced the platitude effortlessly. 'If there had been an accident someone would have phoned, I'm sure. John knew where you would be.'

At this point there was one of those pauses in the general conversation that occur at all parties, and the sound of a ringing telephone in another room was clear. Minutes later a maid appeared; Dr Porter was wanted on the phone. As Alan Porter, waving an apology, went to answer his call, conversations resumed – but not for long. His reappearance brought silence again.

'I'm terribly sorry, Angela, Bernard, everyone. I didn't expect to be on duty this evening, but my colleague is ill and I've been summoned.' He looked at his wife. 'Darling, I'll have to take the car, and I don't know when I'll be back.'

'Not to worry,' Cross said at once. 'We'll see Lorna gets home safely.'

He escorted the doctor to the front door. 'Trouble, Alan?'

Porter nodded. 'Father Le Merle has been killed. John Wessex found him in the sacristy of St Stephen's. I gather it looks as if he's been murdered.'

'Murdered? Le Merle?' Cross was disbelieving. 'But who on earth would want to murder him? He's liked and respected by everyone in Colombury.'

'That's all I know, Bernard, except that Sergeant Donaldson has informed the Thames Valley Police HQ.'

'Can I tell Angela – and warn Deirdre the Brig will be held up? She'll be wondering what's happened to him.'

'Sure. There's no reason why not. It'll be on the news tomorrow, and no doubt splashed across the front pages of the *Courier* on Monday.'

When Alan Porter reached St Stephen's church carrying his doctor's bag, he found a uniformed police officer outside arguing with a young man. He recognized him as Tim Spenser, the son of the editor of the *Courier*, Colombury's daily newspaper. Spenser turned to the doctor with relief.

'Good evening, sir. I'm glad to see you. Perhaps you could persuade this – this officer that I am a bona fide member of the press, and have a right to attend the scene of a crime.'

'How do you know there's been a crime?' Porter enquired.

'A tip-off,' Spenser said. 'I heard Le Merle had been knifed. Your presence would suggest it's true, sir, or are you here to say some prayers?'

Porter ignored the question. 'Let me in,' he said to the police officer.

The man, recognizing Dr Porter as the police surgeon, did as he was asked, but as the doctor passed into the church the journalist pushed in behind him, in spite of the officer's protestations. Porter was mildly surprised to see so few people in the building. There were two more police officers, one a woman, and Sergeant Donaldson, who was standing in front of the altar as if about to bless the three figures in the front pew. These were Brigadier Wessex and Patrick Gough,

18

sitting together and, kneeling at the far end of the pew, Father Hanson, whom Porter knew by sight.

Donaldson came down the two steps from the altar. He frowned at the *Courier*'s representative, but otherwise ignored him although Spenser had already taken a photograph of Father Hanson, and he addressed himself to Porter. 'Ah, there you are, Doctor,' he said, leaving 'at last' to be understood. 'I've called in the top brass as it's clearly a murder case, and Detective Superintendent Tansey is on his way from HQ.'

Pompous ass, Alan Porter thought, but 'Good,' he said mildly. 'Now, where is Father Le Merle?'

'In the sacristy, the vestry.' Donaldson gestured towards the closed door. 'You needn't worry about the handle. It was covered with prints before we arrived and Brigadier Wessex had already inspected the body.'

'How were we to know what we would find when we opened the door?' Gough asked suddenly with surprising aggression. 'Anyway, the killer would have been wearing gloves. He came prepared.'

'You don't *know* that, Mr Gough,' Donaldson said with a degree of contempt.

But Gough was not to be denied. 'I know there wasn't a knife in the sacristy, and a chap wouldn't have been carrying one casual-like when he came to see the priest, would he?'

There was no immediate answer to this, and Porter exchanged glances with the Brigadier before going into the sacristy. In spite of what Donaldson had said he used a handkerchief to open the door. Then he pulled on a pair of surgical gloves and examined the body, moving it as little as possible.

'Well?' Donaldson demanded as Porter finished his examination and came out into the church.

'As you surmised, Sergeant,' Porter said slowly. 'The victim is dead and has been dead for at most two or three hours. I couldn't put a closer time to it than that. However, I suggest we wait for your superiors; I take it they'll include the pathologist. They should be here quite soon.'

19

Nodding as if in dismissal, he went to sit beside Wessex. 'Did you find him – the priest?'

'Yes. Gough and I together.' The brigadier sighed. 'He was a good man, Father Le Merle, too good in some ways. I'm afraid that's why he died.'

'What do you mean, John?'

'Oh, I don't know. I'm talking rubbish. Pay no attention.' Wessex was momentarily irritable.

'You've had a shock,' Porter said gently. 'After all, Le Merle was a friend of yours, wasn't he? And a cold-blooded killing like this is different from death in war, or even on an operating table.' Receiving no response, he continued, 'What I don't understand is what you were doing here. Every-one – including Deirdre – expected you at the Crosses' party.'

'I intended to be there, but I wanted a word with Father. The poor man must have been dead when I got here.'

'I see,' Porter said, though his comment was not strictly accurate and, suddenly aware of someone behind him, he swung round to find his face close to Tim Spenser's. 'Go away, you bloody little eavesdropper,' he hissed.

Spenser laughed, but he moved back. 'See Monday's *Courier*,' he said.

'Good evening, sir,' said Sergeant Donaldson, coming for-ward to greet Detective Superintendent Tansey. Although he wouldn't have admitted it, he was a little scared of this tall, lean, good-looking man, who was one of the senior officers of the Serious Crime Squad of the Thames Valley Police Force. 'An unhappy affair this,' he went on, 'most unhappy. Somehow the fact that the victim was a man of God seems to make the crime worse.'

'Evening, Sergeant,' Tansey said.

He looked about him. He had never been in St Stephen's church before, though he knew Colombury well and had been involved in several cases in and around the town, including one when he had nearly been killed and as a result had spent several weeks in the local hospital. He was glad to see that Porter was already here; he had come to respect the police surgeon as a man of common sense. He recognized Brigadier Wessex, with whom he was acquainted, but he didn't know the other man who was shaking the shoulder of a priest as if to rouse him from deep prayer or from sleep. Spenser, guessing that Tansey would have him removed, had tactfully withdrawn on the superintendent's arrival.

Donaldson introduced Father Hanson and Patrick Gough. Tansey's immediate impression was that the priest looked ill and he wondered what a priest was doing with lipstick on his clerical collar. He asked if anyone else had been in the church.

'At least a hundred, I would guess,' Donaldson said bitterly. 'Brigadier Wessex had sent them all home before I arrived.'

'There clearly wasn't going to be a service,' Wessex said, 'and people have commitments, meals to get, children to fetch and so on. I didn't consider it necessary to keep everyone here for hours. But I take full responsibility.'

Tansey accepted this without comment, but he noted that Wessex was very much on edge, which surprised him a little. He said he had to see Father Le Merle's body, and at once Donaldson started to explain about fingerprints. Tansey brushed him aside. 'Later! Later, Sergeant,' he said, perhaps too sharply, but he had sensed an undercurrent of feeling among those present. Interested, he nevertheless decided to disregard this for the moment, thinking it was probably due to Donaldson's inability, in spite of his efficiency in many ways, to react easily to people. He repeated his request to see Le Merle's body, and this time the sergeant escorted him without demur to the sacristy. After that events seemed to take their own course.

Dr Ghent, the pathologist, arrived in his latest expensive car. He was in evening dress and explained he had been about to go out to dinner. His examination of the body was perfunctory and, annoyed at the interruption to his arrangements, he was not prepared to be particularly helpful.

'I agree with Porter,' he said to Tansey curtly. 'Death took place not more than five hours ago, and probably less. But you'll have to wait for the PM and my report – Tuesday, I expect. I'll let you know.'

As he had blown in, Ghent blew out again. Tansey and Porter exchanged rueful smiles. When Ghent was in one of these moods there was no arguing with him. And by now the Scene of Crime team had arrived under Inspector Whitelaw. When the photographers and fingerprint experts had done their work, the body was removed to a waiting ambulance and the sacristy was subjected to a minute examination.

Since the room was small and the team experienced, scarcely needing the inspector's supervision, Whitelaw joined Tansey, who was talking with the brigadier and Gough. Dr Porter had excused himself and, having called his wife on his mobile phone, was on his way home; he couldn't face a return to the Crosses' party, which he had been shocked to realize was still under way. Sergeant Donaldson and his minions had also departed, except for one officer left at the door to discourage the curious, for a small knot of people, scenting tragedy as if by osmosis, had gathered outside.

Tansey said, 'I'm trying to establish the time of death more closely. I think it's possible. The brigadier says it must have been before 5.45 when he arrived at the church and I'm sure the Misses Blair will confirm this. Now, he saw no one leave and there was –' He paused as Wessex made an inarticulate sound.

'Superintendent, I'm sorry. I've just remembered,' Wessex said. 'I didn't actually see anyone leave, but as the lights came on the door was closing as if someone had just gone out.'

'I see,' said Tansey. 'The Misses Blair might be able to help, perhaps.'

'Perhaps,' Wessex shrugged, 'but I doubt it.'

'And there was no one else in the church?'

Wessex hesitated, but decided he had to tell the truth. 'Only Alfred Yorke. He – he was having his supper. The remains of it is in that pew over there.' He pointed.

'What – having his supper?' Tansey went to look.

Gough came to the brigadier's rescue and gave a fair explanation of Yorke and his eccentric behaviour. 'That's right, isn't it, Father?' he said to Hanson.

22

'Yes. The man's a nuisance, a hopeless case, but –'

'He wouldn't harm Father Le Merle,' Wessex said. 'Why should he? Father was always very good to him.'

'Where does he live, this Alfred Yorke?' Tansey asked, and was surprised when the question was greeted with amusement.

'Here, in St Stephen's, more or less,' Hanson said. 'At least he gives it as his address. In fact, we'd better make sure he's not in one of the confessionals before the church is locked up for the night.'

Superintendent Tansey shook his head in disbelief. In his experience no case in which Colombury was concerned was ever simple, but this one promised to produce more contradictions and absurdities than most. He sighed. For the moment he would stick to the strictly practical aspects of the affair.

'Father Hanson, when did you last see Father Le Merle?' he enquired.

'Lunch – no, tea.' Hanson was vague. 'If we're in, we usually have a cup of tea and a biscuit about four. Father Le Merle came in to the presbytery just as I was leaving.'

'That would be about quarter past, half past four?'

'Nearer four, Superintendent. Today Mrs Faudin, our housekeeper, made me an early cup. I had to go out to visit a sick parishioner. I didn't get back till after six.'

Having given himself an alibi, for no apparent reason the priest blushed deeply, and again Tansey wondered about the lipstick on his collar. But that could wait. The superintendent doubted if Hanson had killed his superior, but his evidence was crucially important. If, as seemed possible, the housekeeper would confirm that Le Merle had been alive at four o'clock, then the priest must have met his death within the next two hours. It was a fairly short space of time and this might well help to find the killer.

Inspector Whitelaw interrupted Tansey's thoughts. 'Father Hanson, there's a safe in the sacristy.'

'Yes. It contains the silver we use in the various religious liturgies,' Hanson said. 'There's no connection between the church and the presbytery, and until the safe was put in, whatever was needed had to be carried all the way round every time.'

'You've checked the contents this evening?' Whitelaw was casual.

'No, I haven't, but it'll be locked.'

'It isn't. It's shut but not locked.'

'And the silver? The silver's gone? Oh, no!' Father Hanson half got to his feet, then collapsed back into his seat. 'The thief must have made Father Le Merle open it and then killed him.'

'Possibly, but, if so, he didn't take much. The safe looks pretty full to me,' Whitelaw said.

Hanson glared at the inspector. 'Then why did you pretend the silver was gone? Are you trying to trick me?'

'Father Hanson, please,' Tansey objected. 'Would you know if something was missing? I think you'll have to come and look. The safe will need to be locked for the night anyway. Have you an inventory?'

'I think there's one in Father Le Merle's study,' Hanson replied.

Reluctantly Hanson stood up again and followed Tansey into the sacristy. The superintendent opened the safe door. He was watching Hanson and he saw the appalled expression that spread across the priest's face.

'The chalice has gone,' Hanson said. 'It's – it's St Stephen's most cherished possession. It dates back to the days when it was illegal to say Mass in England and was given to us by a parishioner when the church was built in 1919. It doesn't look much, but – but it's priceless!'

'Do you think the theft of this chalice is the simple explanation for Le Merle's death?' Whitelaw asked as he and Tansey drove away from Colombury for Oxford and their respective homes.

'No.' Tansey was blunt.

'Why not? Le Merle finds thief in sacristy. That door wouldn't be difficult to force. Thief makes Le Merle open safe, takes chalice and kills the priest because he's been recognized.'

'There was no sign that the sacristy door had been forced. If the priest was already there the light would have warned the thief, and either he wouldn't have gone in or he would have made sure he was unrecognizable. And why just take the chalice, which will be hard to sell if it's as unique as Hanson says? Much easier to get rid of those candlesticks, for instance. And anyway, why not take the lot and just tie up Le Merle? Why risk an unnecessary murder rap? You could be right, Maurice, but somehow I doubt it.'

'But why should anyone deliberately kill a harmless priest?'

'That's one of the questions we have to answer,' Tansey said. 'Perhaps Le Merle wasn't so harmless.'

CHAPTER 3

The next morning when the alarm woke him, Father Hanson turned over and tried to go to sleep again, but it was no use. He knew he had to get up. The police would be here before too long and he had much to do. He must telephone the bishop's secretary – Sunday or not – tell him what had happened, and ask for advice; it had been much too late the previous night. He must contact the two villages where he was due to say Mass later that day, and warn them that he would not be coming. Most importantly, he must get in touch with Father Le Merle's family, who came from the Channel Islands; in the circumstances it had been thought appropriate that the priest rather than the police should break the news to the Le Merles. He must also attend to his own religious duties. And he must take some paracetamol to stop the dreadful throbbing in his head!

Reluctantly he got out of bed and, after a hurried prayer, went along to the bathroom. He took two pills and stared at himself in the mirror over the washbasin. He looked dreadful. Why, oh why, he asked himself, had he drunk all that whisky the previous evening? He must have been, he had been, out of his mind. Normally he wouldn't take more than a small sherry or half a pint of lager, and then only on special occasions.

He washed and shaved, his hand shaking so much that he cut himself twice, and, when on his return to the bedroom he saw the lipstick on his clerical collar, he nearly despaired. He wondered if anyone else had noticed the stain and was quite sure they must have done.

It was a chastened young priest who went down to breakfast. He had broken the news of Father Le Merle's death to

26

Mrs Faudin when she returned from her sister's the night before, and she had not cried at the time, but now her eyes were red with weeping. And both priest and housekeeper were horribly conscious of the empty chair where Father Le Merle had always sat at the head of the table.

However, Mrs Faudin had prepared the usual breakfast and, though Hanson was not in the least hungry, he forced himself to eat, hoping the food would ease his aching head. He couldn't think how he was going to survive the day.

Meanwhile, Superintendent Tansey made some phone calls from his headquarters and arrived in Colombury shortly after ten o'clock. He went straight to St Stephen's presbytery. He was accompanied by Detective Sergeant Abbot, who was a colleague of long standing and, as much as their difference in rank allowed, a good friend. Inspector Whitelaw was following with the mobile incident van which would be parked behind the police station.

To the annoyance of Father Hanson, who had opened the door to Tansey and Abbot and ushered them into a dark and gloomy parlour that smelt strongly of furniture polish, the superintendent demanded to interview Mrs Faudin first. She was a small, bird-like woman, a widow of many years, and she sat on the edge of the chair that Abbot had drawn up for her. But she was more than willing to talk, and she was clearly oblivious of any implications in what she might be saying, or any suspicions that might be aroused by her words.

'Yes, sir, that's correct,' she affirmed. 'I took Father Hanson his tea sharp at four, or a little before. I think he hoped to be finished and gone before Father Le Merle returned. They'd been having an argument earlier on. You know how it is.'

'Not really, Mrs Faudin. How is it?'

'Two men, living together, working hard and having few pleasures, one of them an easy-going, broad-minded, truly charitable man, the other not long out of the seminary and determined not to bend the smallest rule.'

'Yes, it can't be easy,' Tansey agreed. 'What was the argument about this time?'

Mrs Faudin shrugged. 'As far as I could tell, the usual, sir,

27

the old tramp, Alfred Yorke – not that he really is old. It's just a manner of speaking, and it's not as if some of the parishioners don't agree with Father Hanson. But from what I heard, which wasn't much, because I was in a hurry to get off to my sister's, it was a – a bitter argument. Father Le Merle, that is, sounded right angry, which isn't like him, but then he's not been himself lately.'

She stopped abruptly. 'Oh dear, I don't know what I'm saying. I shouldn't be gossiping about the poor man like this, and him dead, murdered in his own church.' She started to cry. 'If only I'd known when I took in his tea I wasn't going to see him again.'

Tansey allowed her a moment to control herself, then he said gently, 'Mrs Faudin, what did you mean by remarking that Father Le Merle hadn't been himself lately?'

'I – I'm not sure I know, sir. He's been a little . . . short-tempered would be too strong a word, but he's been a mite irritable, as if he was worrying about something. And he's not been eating well,' she concluded triumphantly.

'That sounds a very good description,' Tansey said encouragingly. 'Is there anything else you can tell us that might be a help?'

'I don't think –' she began. Then, 'Well, there was the time I dropped the chalice, the one Father Hanson says has been stolen. It's very old and very valuable. I was cleaning it and it slipped out of my hands on to the kitchen floor. Father was terribly kind. I was afraid I might have dented it or scratched it, but he said the oddest thing, he said, "Damage to material things can be easily forgiven. It's when someone precious is harmed that it can be next to impossible to forgive whoever is responsible. Nevertheless, one has to try." At the time it seemed to me an odd remark, and he sounded terribly sad as he said it, sir.'

Tansey nodded in sympathy, though he thought that Mrs Faudin was probably reading too much into a simple comment. 'Thank you very much, Mrs Faudin. You've been most helpful. I think that's all for the moment. Would you be good enough to ask Father Hanson to have a word with us?'

'Yes, sir. That I will.'

She bustled out and Tansey said, 'What did you make of her, Abbot? You're a pretty good judge.'

Sergeant Abbot, who had remained silent throughout the interview, said at once, 'A nice woman. Reliable. Father Le Merle was alive at 4.15. It's a pity she went off to her sister's then, or we might have the exact time he went across to the church.'

'Can't have everything. She produced two interesting facts. Le Merle has been worried recently, and he and Hanson didn't get on too well.'

'I would say she's prejudiced in Le Merle's favour, sir.'

'Yes. I agree.'

Tansey gave Abbot a warning glance as the door opened and Father Hanson came in. He had not knocked. He was looking pale but composed. He sat down immediately without waiting for an invitation; after all, it was his parlour and his presbytery. Tansey decided to attempt to shake him.

'It would seem, Father Hanson, that apart from the killer you were the last person to see Father Le Merle alive.'

'Why – why do you say that?'

'According to Mrs Faudin, you and Father Le Merle were having tea when she went out. Is that true?'

'Ye-es, but I left soon after. I had to visit an elderly parishioner who is – is chronically ill. He – they live over beyond Little Chipping.'

'Thank you. Their names and the address, please.'

Father Hanson provided the required information, and Abbot made a show of taking it down. Tansey didn't doubt that the visit would be confirmed, but he wondered why Hanson should suddenly seem so embarrassed and ill at ease. He allowed a silence to lengthen.

'I – I had only been back here for a few minutes when Patrick Gough came over from the church and told me the dreadful news about Father Le Merle.'

'You had had a quarrel – an argument, say – with Father Le Merle?' Tansey pressed.

'Ah. Mrs Faudin again.' Hanson almost sneered. 'Was she listening at the door?'

29

Tansey ignored the question. 'The argument was about Alfred Yorke and the way he behaves in the church. Is that right?'

Hanson drew a deep breath and gave a half smile. 'Yes, that's right, Superintendent. Yorke is an almighty menace. In my opinion he should be in a mental home or in prison. One of these days he'll commit a real crime.'

'Do you think he might have killed Father Le Merle?'

'He's more likely to have wanted to kill me.'

Hanson spoke with assurance. His nervousness had vanished, at least temporarily, and mentally Tansey kicked himself. It was obvious that he had missed something – some thread. He changed the subject abruptly.

'Have you managed to contact Father Le Merle's relations yet?' he asked.

'I tried,' Hanson said. 'Mr Le Merle – Father Le Merle's brother – and his wife are touring in France. I spoke to their nineteen-year-old son, who sounded very sensible. He said he didn't know exactly where his parents were, but when they phoned, which they almost certainly would in the next day or two, he would break the news to them.'

'Right. That's fine,' Tansey said. 'It's always possible that they'll learn about it from the radio or an English newspaper, and anyway there's nothing they can do at the moment. Now I'd like to search Father Le Merle's room.'

'Search it?' Hanson was taken aback. 'I – I'm not sure.'

'You don't need to be sure, Father Hanson. This is a murder case. It's probable that Father Le Merle was killed by someone he knew. Of course, the killer might have been a casual thief, but in my opinion that's unlikely. In any event we need to look through Father Le Merle's private papers, his correspondence, and so on. I assume he has such things. From my observation, neither you nor Father Le Merle belong to a strict monastic order, and I don't require your bishop's permission.'

Hanson staggered as he got to his feet. His face flushed, and then became very pale. He seemed to have difficulty in speaking. Sergeant Abbot coughed and cleared his throat loudly, his usual warning signal that the superintendent was pressing a potential witness too hard.

'I don't have a search warrant, Father Hanson,' Tansey continued. 'It's not easy on a Sunday, but I expected your co-operation, though naturally, if you insist –'

'No! No, that won't be necessary.' Hanson had found his voice. 'If you'll wait a minute, I'll get Mrs Faudin to show you, Superintendent.'

Father Le Merle's room was a fair size and less depressing than the parlour, but it was nothing if not austere. It contained a divan bed, a cupboard with hanging space and drawers, a desk, two chairs – one upright, one moderately comfortable – and behind a screen a hand basin, above which was an almost empty medicine cabinet with a mirror for a door. There was a worn strip of carpet on the floor, and in a corner, under a crucifix, a prie-dieu.

And the room lacked colour. All the furnishings were a greyish-brown, and there was no brightness anywhere. Even when Sergeant Abbot opened the drab curtains, he revealed only a view of a car park. He opened the cupboard and began to go through the clothes; Father Le Merle had not possessed a large wardrobe, and one shelf was given up to devotional books, from which fluttered a handful of holy cards. The missal on the prie-dieu was equally unhelpful, but Abbot persevered.

Meanwhile Superintendent Tansey had seated himself at the desk. Quickly he learnt that Paul Le Merle had been a methodical man, for everything was neatly filed: bills due or receipted, letters answered or awaiting answers, engagements. But that was about all Tansey did learn. Father Le Merle appeared to have no private life, though his family in Jersey kept in fairly close touch with him. Otherwise, he was apparently concerned only with his church and his parishioners – presumably a harmless priest whom no one would want to kill.

'Sir!' Abbot broke in on Tansey's musings. 'I've found a photograph. I nearly missed it because it didn't fall out when I shook the book. It was tucked under the cover.'

'What sort of photograph?' Tansey half hoped Abbot would reply that it was of a naked dancing girl.

'A young lady,' Abbot said. He brought the small print over to Tansey and put it down on the desk. 'It's only a snapshot, but a good one.'

Tansey regarded it with interest. This was, he supposed, someone who had once been important to Paul Le Merle, or he wouldn't have kept her picture. Not a sister. A close friend? A lover? There was neither name nor date on the back.

She was a pretty girl – about twenty, Tansey guessed – not beautiful but attractive, with dark curly hair, large brown eyes and a wide smile. She was of medium height and had good legs; she was wearing a very short skirt, but Tansey was well aware that this was a fashion fad that came and went and wasn't a reliable guide to the date of the photograph. Nevertheless, he was inclined to place it at some time in the sixties.

'Abbot, why did you call her "a young lady"?' he asked suddenly.

Abbot laughed. 'I really don't know, sir. It's what came to mind when I looked at her likeness. There's something about her, the way she's standing, perhaps, that suggests a sort of assurance combined with a certain modesty.'

It was Tansey's turn to laugh. 'Modesty? In spite of the display of legs?' he queried.

But he knew what Abbot meant, though he wouldn't have described the girl in those particular terms. She gave the impression – at any rate to him – of being both self-possessed and at the same time contradictorily insecure, an introvert for sure. Then he scorned his own assessment. Who were he or Abbot to form judgements of someone's character from a snap, probably taken at an idle moment, though cherished? He took one of Le Merle's envelopes and slipped the photograph inside, initialling the flap and asking Abbot to do the same. Strangely enough the print was making the priest more real to him.

'We'll take this, Sergeant. Your can bear witness as to where it was found.'

32

'Yes, sir.' Abbot looked doubtful. 'Are you going to show it to Father Hanson?'

'Definitely not! We don't mention it, not for the present, not to anyone. You understand?' Tansey bit off the words.

'Yes, sir.'

It was not often that the superintendent spoke so sharply and so authoritatively to Abbot, but the sergeant didn't resent it. He knew Tansey too well. He knew that the suppressed anger had not been directed towards himself, but against the superintendent's own feeling of frustration. Why the superintendent should feel this way he had no idea, but he sympathized.

'What next, sir?' he asked.

Tansey hesitated. Then, 'Let's get out of this depressing place,' he said. 'It may be all right for a priest, but it doesn't suit me. We'll go and see what Inspector Whitelaw has managed to find out.'

Maurice Whitelaw had been busy. On arriving in Colombury – a sleepy place so early on a Sunday morning – an hour after Tansey, he had parked the incident van in the car park behind the police station, made sure the telephone engineers were on hand, set the technical officers to their tasks and walked round to the station to see Sergeant Donaldson.

Donaldson, who had been on duty since six that morning and was determined to show his efficiency, gave the inspector a chilly welcome. He had nothing to report, and resented the fact.

'We can't do the impossible, sir,' he said, anticipating rebuke. 'My men have checked all Alfred Yorke's old haunts, but he's not to be found. He could be up in the woods. It would need a regiment to search them thoroughly. But it's my belief the bugger left Colombury last night once he learned the priest was dead, that is, if he didn't kill him.'

'Why should he have killed him?' Whitelaw asked mildly. 'As I understand it, Father Le Merle was very kind to him.'

'Maybe Le Merle caught him pinching that chalice and he panicked and knifed him.' Donaldson shrugged. 'Anyway, we'll go on looking for him, sir.'

'You do that,' Whitelaw said.

It had been an unsatisfactory conversation and the inspector was not pleased when, on leaving Donaldson's room, he found Tim Spenser of the *Courier* propping up the counter in the outer office. The previous year the *Courier*, by running a hate campaign against him in the course of investigations into another case, had almost lost him his job, and only Tansey's intervention had saved him. Nevertheless, he greeted Spenser pleasantly; whatever the provocation, it didn't pay to be too stroppy with the local press.

'Good morning,' he said. 'I was coming to see you later. There's an advert we'd like you to put in tomorrow's papers and, if you'll take it and hand it in to the right department, it'll save me a visit to your establishment.'

'Sure,' Spenser said. 'Why not? Anything to help the police.'

'It's pretty vague,' Whitelaw admitted, producing the copy from his pocket. 'It just requests anyone who might have information relevant to Father Le Merle's death to ring that number, but it does give a good description of the chalice that's missing.'

'Fine!' Spenser said. 'We know where to charge it,' he added mischievously.

While they were talking they had walked out of the police station together. Now Spenser threw his leg over his motorbike, which he had parked outside. He grinned at Whitelaw.

'With luck the nurse who was in such a hurry to get away from St Stephen's will answer your advert,' he said, 'but somehow I doubt it.'

'What the –' Whitelaw began, and swore softly as Spenser roared away, lifting an arm in salute.

'No, I don't know what the bloody man was talking about,' Whitelaw said later to Tansey, 'and he gave me no chance to ask him. I could scarcely run after his motorbike, could I?'

The superintendent was careful not to smile at Whitelaw's indignation. 'There may be nothing in it,' he remarked. 'Spenser may have made up the story to rile us. He'd love to send us on a wild goose chase. It would be his idea of a

black joke, and it would be damned difficult to prove he was
obstructing the police in the course of their inquiries.'

'You may be right,' Whitelaw said, pacified, though still
unsatisfied.

CHAPTER 4

Superintendent Tansey and Inspector Whitelaw sat in a corner of the bar at the Windrush Arms; Sergeant Abbot, who was a native of Colombury, had gone to have Sunday dinner with his parents. It was an amicable arrangement.

A sudden silence had greeted the entry of Tansey and Whitelaw to the pub. The two detectives were both well known by sight and, though normally none of the locals would have invited himself to join them, there had never been any animosity shown to them; usually they were ignored. But today, beer and sandwiches before them, they were conscious of being the centre of attention. There was a whispering and shuffling among the other drinkers, and doubtful glances were thrown at them.

'What do you think their trouble is?' Whitelaw muttered.

'Can't imagine. Just disregard them,' said Tansey, taking a large bite from a sandwich. 'Excellent ham, this.'

Whitelaw nodded agreement and tried to concentrate on the food and drink on the table, but his eyes kept wandering to a group who seemed to be arguing among themselves. Then they appeared to reach a decision.

'Couple of them are coming over to us,' he said.

'So I see,' Tansey replied, continuing to eat. 'Yes?' He looked up as the men – one was scarcely more than a boy – reached them.

'Sir,' said the older of the two. 'We don't want to bother you, and we may be wasting your time, but it did say on the radio that the police would be grateful for any information that could lead to Father Le Merle's murderer. We were all right fond of the Father, you know, and we'd want to help if we could. I'm Mat Brown and this is Jason Clark.'

'You're both members of St Stephen's congregation?' Tansey probed.

'Oh no, sir! We're not Romans. We're chapel. But that makes no difference to what we feel about Father Le Merle and it made no difference to him neither. When the recession was really bad in the town he used to give parties for the kids – any kids – and he'd drop off bags of food where he knew it was most needed. We all thought he was a really good man. Why anyone should want to kill him is a fair mystery.'

'One I hope to solve,' Tansey said drily. 'And you implied you had some information, Mr Brown.'

'Not me. Jason here.'

'Fine. Inspector Whitelaw will get you both a pint and you can tell me about it.'

'Thank you, sir. Just a half for Jason. He's not much of a drinker.'

Jason, unlike his companion, wasn't much of a talker either, but gradually his story was prised out of him, including the fact that he had that evening collected a birthday cake from the Gronskis, who owned the Pomme d'Or, a superior local restaurant. By coincidence, Inspector Whitelaw, who had met Gronski's daughter, Hazel, in the course of a previous case in Colombury, had fallen in love with her and eventually had married her.

In any case, Jason's tale was not particularly helpful, though it was obvious that he had seen a tall man in a raincoat leaving St Stephen's Church some time around five-thirty, and ten to fifteen minutes later on his way back he had seen someone who he took to be the same man going up the steps into the church. He was vague about times but the more he was questioned, the more positive he became that it was the same man, though he admitted that on neither occasion had he seen the man's face.

'And a moment or two after the guy went in again, the lights in the church came on,' he suddenly volunteered. 'The windows all lit up.'

The detectives, who had been inclined to discount the whole story, swiftly became interested. They refrained from

37

looking at each other; they knew their thoughts were identical. Brigadier Wessex, who was a tall man and had been wearing a raincoat, had turned on the lights in the church minutes after he had arrived – but had he been there before?

'You've no idea who he was?' Tansey said. 'Have you ever seen him around the town?'

Jason shook his head. 'It was dark. The street's not well lit there and I didn't see him properly. He was just a shape.'

'So you couldn't swear it was the same man?'

'Swear? No.' Jason didn't like the idea of swearing to anything. 'But I'm jolly sure he was.'

Obviously nothing was going to shake the youth in his belief, and the superintendent decided not to press him further. He thanked him and Mat Brown to indicate that their talk was finished, and didn't take the hint when Brown looked ruefully at his empty tankard.

As Brown reluctantly stood up to leave, Whitelaw said to Jason, 'I suppose you didn't see anyone else near the church? One of the nurses from the hospital, perhaps?'

'A nurse. No, I didn't see no nurse.' Jason shook his head firmly. 'There were two old ladies – I think they were old by the way they went up the steps careful-like – and then the man came just behind them. Nobody else.'

'What did you make of all that, Maurice?' Tansey asked as the two officers left the Windrush Arms and strolled towards the police station to fetch their car.

'I believe young Jason was telling the truth as he saw it,' Whitelaw said at once. 'The two old ladies were obviously the Misses Blair, who, we hope, will confirm Brigadier Wessex's story that he arrived at 5.45 approximately, close behind them, and immediately went to put on the lights. We shall have to ask him whether he'd been in the church earlier that evening. I expect him to deny it.'

'Why?'

'Because I think it's a fair assumption that whoever left the church earlier, about 5.30, was Father Le Merle's killer. Don't you agree?'

'Not necessarily, but it's not improbable. The time would

fit. The killer couldn't expect the priest to arrive there extra early merely to suit him. However, this odd character, Alfred Yorke, who seems to cause so much controversy by squatting in the church, can't be ruled out.'

'No motive,' Whitelaw said.

'We've not found anyone yet who has a motive of any kind, not one that would stand up in court at any rate. People seem to have disagreed with Father Le Merle, but no one has actually spoken ill of him – rather the reverse. He was probably regarded as a pain in the neck by some locals, but he's not an obvious victim, as far as I can see at present.'

'The theft of the chalice?' Whitelaw queried. 'Le Merle tried to save it?'

'Why choose to nick an article that would be difficult to sell? Remember, the safe was open. There was other equally valuable stuff – or stuff that would have seemed equally valuable to someone like Yorke – for the taking.'

'If it were Yorke, he might not want to sell it. He seems a strange individual. On the other hand, it would take a cold-blooded character to stick a knife in someone who had been kind to you, then wait around until his body was found.'

'Killer or not, we certainly want to talk to Yorke,' Tansey said firmly. 'If he doesn't turn up soon, we'll have to organize a search for him as a material witness.'

By now they had reached the police station car park. They looked in on the officers in the incident van, but the men had nothing to report, and were busy playing a game of poker. Tansey told them to cheer up; they wouldn't be bored once the *Courier* hit the streets next day.

'At least I hope they won't be,' he said to Whitelaw as they set off to see Brigadier Wessex; he had made an appointment on the phone that morning. 'I think we're going to need all the input we can get from the public.'

Brigadier and Mrs Wessex were having coffee after lunch. Deirdre looked anxiously at her husband. He had eaten hardly anything and was now gazing into the fire while his coffee grew cold.

'John, what's the matter?' she asked at last. 'I know you're upset about Father Le Merle's death. We all are. And it must have been horrible for you and Patrick Gough finding him, but –'

'Oh, Deirdre, do shut up. Please. You've talked of nothing else since yesterday.'

'Is that so surprising? At least I haven't talked about it in my sleep.'

'What the hell do you mean by that?' Wessex was startled and angry.

'Don't be so irritable!' Worried, Deirdre snapped in return. 'It's true. You kept me awake, muttering, "I wish I'd never done it. I wish I'd never done it." Done what, John?'

'Quarrelled with Father Le Merle over that wretched man, Yorke. I rather lost my temper. That's why I wanted to catch him before Mass – to apologize – but of course I never got the chance.'

'I see.' Deirdre wasn't sure whether to believe her husband or not, but at that moment the doorbell rang, preventing her from asking more questions.

'That will be the police,' Wessex said. 'For God's sake, Deirdre, don't mention to Tansey that I've been talking in my sleep.'

'No, I won't.' She looked at him for reassurance, but received none. 'I'll take out the coffee tray if you'll let them in.' She hadn't intended to meet the police officers, as she hadn't been to St Stephen's the previous evening and could tell them nothing, but now she changed her mind and returned to the drawing room.

'Good afternoon, Mrs Wessex,' Tansey said, rising from the chair to which the brigadier had waved him. 'We're sorry to intrude on you on a Sunday, but this is a serious case and we're going to need all the help we can get.'

'I'm afraid you won't get much from me,' she said. 'I was at a party, where John should have been too. I was very worried when he didn't arrive.'

Tansey smiled at her. He rather liked Deirdre Wessex. She

40

was a thin, nervous woman, considerably younger than her husband, and he guessed that theirs was a second marriage. But the brigadier, he thought, was looking somewhat jaundiced today, and he sensed a certain tension between the couple. He wondered why Wessex had frowned at his wife's remark, which had appeared innocent enough. On a hunch he decided to follow it up.

'This was the party given by Mr and Mrs Cross,' he said. 'They're neighbours of yours, I believe. You went straight to their house, Mrs Wessex, but your husband went into Colombury. Why was that, sir?'

'I had business in town.'

'With Father Le Merle?' Whitelaw asked.

'No – yes. I mean I had business with my lawyer, James Petty of Petty & Schofield. We're trying to buy some land that adjoins our garden. And as I was there I thought I would have a word with Father Le Merle.'

'Although it meant you would probably be late for this party?' Tansey said.

'I didn't expect to be *very* late.' Wessex was clearly puzzled by the direction of the questions. 'I don't understand –'

'What time did you leave your lawyer, sir?'

'Just before five, I think, but –'

'And you reached St Stephen's – when?'

'At about 5.45, as I said. As the Misses Blair will verify. What is this, Superintendent? You can't suspect me of killing Father Le Merle, surely?'

Deirdre Wessex gave a high-pitched laugh which caused the three men to stare at her. 'Sorry,' she said, 'but it was such a stupid suggestion. My husband's a good Catholic, Superintendent. The last person he'd kill would be his priest.'

Ignoring this intervention, Whitelaw said, 'Was that the first time that evening you had been in St Stephen's, sir?'

'Yes! It most certainly was,' Wessex said shortly. 'I will explain. After I left Petty's I sat in my car until I thought Father Le Merle would probably be in the sacristy; it was his custom to be there a while before the evening Mass. You see, I had had a difference of opinion with him over the tramp, Alfred Yorke, and I fear I had expressed myself rather

41

forcibly. I wanted to apologize. After all, as my wife says, he is my priest, and St Stephen's is his church.'

'Thank you, Brigadier. Thank you, sir,' Tansey said. 'I'm sorry to probe so much, but I'm sure you understand. This Yorke character seems to be a real nuisance – to the police and everyone else. How long has he been living in Colombury?'

'About two to three years.' Wessex looked at his wife for confirmation. He was clearly relieved that the questioning had taken a new slant. 'To say he lives in Colombury is somewhat inaccurate. He has no house. He dosses down where he thinks he will. He seems to prefer it that way, though heaps of people have tried to help him.'

'And he was in the church yesterday evening when you put the lights on?'

'Yes, but nuisance as he was, I can't believe he would have killed Father Le Merle or stolen the chalice.'

'Nevertheless,' Whitelaw said, 'he seems to have disappeared.'

'He does from time to time, especially recently,' Deirdre Wessex said quickly. 'He comes and goes. I suppose you might call him a free spirit.'

Laughing about it later, Tansey and Whitelaw agreed that there were many other descriptions of Alfred Yorke that Brigadier Wessex would have preferred to offer. They also agreed that the brigadier had not told them the whole truth, and that both he and his wife had been unnecessarily anxious or at least uncertain.

'He denied seeing anyone in the street, except the Misses Blair, who were going into the church, but that youth Jason saw him as well as the old ladies,' Whitelaw said, 'so shouldn't he have seen Jason?'

'I don't know. Perhaps not,' Tansey said. 'We'll have to find out what the ladies have to say.'

The Misses Blair, however, could not agree about Jason. The taller, thinner, Miss Joan denied having seen anyone except Brigadier Wessex. The shorter, fatter, Miss Jean thought she had seen a young person along the street – at least it was a slight figure and she had taken it to be a girl.

'They all wear these dreadful jeans these days, you know,' she said, smiling sweetly at Tansey. 'You can't tell them apart.'

But about the brigadier, there was no dispute. 'Such a nice, kind man,' they said in chorus. He had put the lights on and they had seen that disreputable tramp having his supper in one of the pews. The dear brigadier was quite right; something needed to be done about this dirty old man, who was a disgrace to St Stephen's.

When the flood of words ceased momentarily, Tansey said quickly, 'Did you see anyone else in the church, catch even a glimpse – Brigadier Wessex had the impression that someone was leaving as he turned on the lights.'

'If the brigadier says it was so, then it was,' said Miss Jean, and her sister nodded in support.

Tansey repressed a sigh, but he persevered, aware that Whitelaw was trying not to grin. 'Ladies, this is an important question, so please think carefully before you answer it. Did anyone – anyone – go into the sacristy between the time the lights came on and Brigadier Wessex went in with Patrick Gough?'

Miss Jean regarded Tansey coldly. 'Superintendent, we are not stupid. Please don't be so patronizing. We would both be prepared to swear on oath that no one – no one – entered the sacristy during that period. And if you imagine that anyone – anyone – could have dashed in there, knifed Father Le Merle and come out again without us being aware of the fact, you must be out of your mind.'

For once in his life Superintendent Richard Tansey was speechless, but this would only have been apparent to someone like Whitelaw who knew him well. 'You misjudge me, ladies,' he said coolly at last. 'I am seeking *confirmation* of the times – in this case the last possible time – between which the murder must have taken place. So thanks very much for your help.'

The detectives stood, Whitelaw a fraction more slowly than Tansey, and allowed themselves to be ushered from the house. Once outside they grinned broadly at each other.

43

'Phew!' Tansey said. 'It's a long time since I've been told off like that.'

'You never asked them if they'd seen a nurse,' Whitelaw said, laughing.

'I think she's a myth,' Tansey said, 'but she might have been the mysterious character who slipped through the door as the lights went on in the church.'

The afternoon was drawing in. The two officers had had a late night and a tiring day. With no weekend rest, a further long week stretched ahead of them, with the fear which always accompanied a murder case that the killer would strike again. They would gladly have called it a day and set off for home; there was still an hour's drive ahead of them. But you didn't reach senior rank in the Thames Valley Police Serious Crime Squad by cutting corners.

'Patrick Gough,' Whitelaw said; it wasn't a question.

'Yes,' Tansey agreed. 'Luckily he lives in the town, in one of those council houses that used to be on the outskirts of Colombury, but have become absorbed over the years. It's near where the Abbots live, so we can pick up the sergeant after we've seen Gough, check with our chaps in the incident van, who are probably still bored stiff and playing cards, and then make for home. Tomorrow, as they say, is another day.'

'Right,' Whitelaw said. 'Patrick Gough, here we come. Let's hope he doesn't keep us long, though I could do with a cuppa if offered.'

Gough didn't disappoint. There was tea, and the remains of a sumptuous cake from the Pomme d'Or. 'My mother loves sweet things,' he said, half apologetically. 'And why shouldn't she? She has few pleasures.'

'Of course. Why not?' Tansey said. 'But now for some questions, I'm afraid.'

'I'm ready,' Gough said. Though nervous, he was eager to help, and he did his best to co-operate, but he had nothing to add to what they already knew.

'I'm sorry,' he said. 'If I'd been five minutes earlier getting to the church – and I would have been if I'd not met Mike Carson as I was about to turn into the lane – you know, the one beside St Stephen's – then I might have seen something

44

useful. As it was I stood chatting to him, and there was already a trickle of people going into the church by the time I got there.'

'Who's Mike Carson?' Tansey asked, more out of politeness than curiosity, as he and Whitelaw were on the point of leaving.

'He works at the *Courier*. A junior editor. He's a good chap, but a dreadful talker. If a girl hadn't come running out of the lane and bumped into us, I'd have been there another ten minutes.' Gough grinned.

'A girl?' Tansey said sharply.

'A nurse?' Whitelaw said.

'Yes,' Gough agreed, surprised. 'She was a nurse. She had on one of those cloaks they wear, but no cap. She was probably late for her shift, which was why she was in such a hurry.' But he could give no more of a description of her, and with that Tansey had to be content.

'At least we now know the nurse is not a myth,' Tansey said as they drove away, 'and we know how Mr Spenser of the *Courier* learnt about her.'

45

CHAPTER 5

Monday dawned, wet and windy. It was to be a frustrating day for everyone connected with the death of Father Le Merle, not least for Bernard Cross.

Cross stared out of the window of his office in the Colombury General Hospital at the rain sluicing to one side down the panes of glass. Automatically he drew a pad towards him and made a note; blocked gutter to be attended to. His thoughts were elsewhere, on Superintendent Tansey and the nurses – or rather on a particular nurse, who might or might not have seen Father Le Merle's murderer. He had forgotten about his appointment with Lance Ritchie.

'Bernard, I'm interrupting you. Your secretary said to go in, but if it's inconvenient I can easily make it another time.'

'No, no! You had an appointment to discuss your schedules and I refuse to fall too far behind with my regular business just to satisfy a whim of the police.'

Ritchie sat in the chair to which Cross had waved him and stretched out his long legs. 'The police?' he said. 'Are they hounding you? Why?' He sounded relaxed and amused and momentarily Bernard Cross disliked him intensely; it was easy for consultants to despise management, he thought, but let them try to run a hospital – a far more difficult task than managing a hotel – and then they wouldn't be so damned superior.

'They've learnt that there was a nurse – her cloak betrayed her – in the vicinity of the crime and at the appropriate time. She may have information helpful to the police inquiry.' Cross tried to equal Ritchie's nonchalance, but his frustration showed through his words. 'Doubtless they're following up innumerable other characters who were around then, and doubtless this is essential – but I wish the bloody girl had been in civvies.'

Ritchie laughed. 'I don't understand the problem.'

'The problem for us here is to accede to Detective Superintendent Tansey's latest stupid request. He wants a complete list of all our nurses who are Roman Catholics, and what shifts they were on that Saturday.'

'Is that so difficult? Surely you must have their details on computer.'

'Religion, yes – and heaven knows what else in the way of personal and private particulars, but shift personnel change by the day – almost by the hour. A nurse is ill – there's a lot of 'flu around at the moment – or there's an emergency in a ward or an accident, which means extra demand for staff in A & E – we used to call it casualty.'

'Tough,' said Ritchie, not without sympathy.

'And if the girl doesn't turn up as an RC, Tansey will next want the dope on every single nurse,' Cross said resignedly. 'Even with computerization it's a time-consuming task.'

'What I don't understand is why the police don't simply ask the girl to come forward.'

'There was a request on the local radio and in today's *Courier* for anyone who might conceivably be able to help to get in touch with the police. But Tansey thinks she may be scared, and he doesn't want to waste time. Hence the lists.'

'Why should she be scared?'

Cross hesitated, regretting what he had said. Tansey had asked him not to spread it around, but already several people knew; one more could scarcely matter. 'In confidence, Lance,' he said, 'John Wessex believes someone left the church as he turned the lights on, and it's possible it was this nurse, in which case she may have seen the murderer in the light given by the banks of candles. Mind you, this is all supposition.'

'Quite.' Ritchie sounded slightly bored.

'Of course, you didn't know Father Le Merle,' Cross said, 'but he was always a welcome visitor to the hospital and was greatly liked – I almost said loved – by everyone here. His death – and such a death – has shaken us all and has spread a pall of gloom over the whole place. I hate to think what will happen when the police start to question the nurses. I may well have a riot on my hands.'

Ritchie laughed. 'Cheer up,' he said. 'I'm sure even the dumbest detective wouldn't suspect one of your nurses of killing this priest.'

Detective Superintendent Richard Tansey was not a dumb detective, and no one at the Thames Valley Police head-quarters, from St John Cowan, the Chief Constable – known behind his back as 'Holy Cow' – to the lowest PC Plod, would have dreamt of suggesting such a thing. No one could win them all, but Tansey's success rate was better than most and his reputation was high. Moreover, and this couldn't always be said of senior police officers, he was generally liked.

On this unpleasant Monday morning, however, Detective Inspector Whitelaw was not feeling kindly disposed towards his superior. Tansey had ordained that Whitelaw should spend the day at the hospital studying lists of nurses' shifts and interviewing the girls. It was a time-consuming, frustrating job, and by lunch he had talked to almost all the nurses registered as Roman Catholics – there had been more than he expected, mostly Irish – without learning anything of interest.

'There was one girl whom, I admit, I distrusted,' he said to Tansey. The superintendent had joined him at the hospital, where Cross had arranged for lunch to be brought to the small room he had allocated to them. 'She herself has a watertight alibi, but I suspect she knows or guesses who the nurse we want might be. Her name is Gemma Drayton, and I think she should be seen again.'

'Right! Maurice, this is precisely why I wanted you to do this job, which, on the face of it, any half-trained officer could do. I hoped that discerning mind of yours would spot some discrepancy, some oddity, in what was said.'

'I could be wrong.' But Whitelaw was pleased.

'Of course, that goes without saying.'

'And you'd like me to spend the rest of the day on the non-Romans? Cross produced this other list.'

'I'm afraid so.' Tansey swallowed the last of his apple pie and poured himself some coffee. 'You said earlier that several girls were ill. What have you done about them?'

'I arranged for Sergeant Donaldson to send WPC Gray to the nurses' home. She's a sensible woman, and her report clears them.'

'Good. Then when we've finished our coffee, we'll send for Nurse Drayton again.'

Gemma Drayton was an attractive girl with auburn hair and wide blue eyes. She was extremely nervous, but was doing her best not to show it. As a result her manner was aggressive.

'I told this policeman all I know this morning,' she said as soon as Tansey had introduced himself. 'It wasn't much. The ward sister, Miss Bascombe, will vouch that I was on duty from four o'clock and I never left the ward. We were far too busy. So what is it you want now?'

'How long have you been at this hospital, Miss Drayton?'

She stared at Tansey. 'A year.'

'Time to make friends among the other nurses. Have you any particular friend?'

She shrugged. 'No. It's too difficult. Our shifts are always changing, and what with emergencies and nurses being off sick, you never know who you'll be on duty with. But I get on very well with everyone.'

She's talking too much, Tansey thought. He said, 'You're Irish, aren't you, Miss Drayton. Do any of the other nurses here come from the same part of the country as you?'

'No. I come from Fermoy; it's not far from Cork.'

'You knew Father Le Merle?'

'Yes and no. That is, I go to his church and he's heard my confession once or twice, but I didn't know him personally, just to say good-day, in fact.'

'I see.' Tansey was running out of questions.

'Okay, Miss Drayton. That's fine.' Tansey smiled at her. 'Thank you for your help. Goodbye.'

'What help?'

Tansey ignored the query. He turned to Whitelaw and began to talk in a low voice about that afternoon's work. Half reluctantly, Gemma Drayton left them.

'Well, that didn't get us very far,' Tansey said as the door closed behind her. 'But I agree with you. She's hiding something. It may be relevant or it may not. At least we've given her some food for thought, and she may change her mind and decide to talk.'

'And perhaps my afternoon's efforts will produce something,' Whitelaw said, but he was not optimistic, and justifiably.

Superintendent Tansey had decided to do some checking on Father Hanson. He collected Sergeant Abbot from the incident van and instructed him to drive to Little Chipping. They were, he said, going to call on Bill Sutton, who was a chronic invalid, and his wife, Belle, who cared for him. The Suttons lived at Lavender Cottage, a little way out of the village. Hanson claimed to have spent the early part of Saturday evening with them, presumably giving spiritual sustenance to Bill. But Tansey hadn't forgotten the lipstick on the clerical collar or the priest's embarrassment when he mentioned the Suttons.

It was not the best afternoon for a drive. The rain had become heavy and the windscreen wipers were straining to perform their task. The lanes were slippery with wet leaves, and fallen branches set traps. But Abbot was a superb driver, and he had been born and brought up in Colombury, so that every turn and twist of the countryside roads in the area was familiar to him. Tansey sat back in his seat and relaxed.

'Did you pick up any information or local gossip this morning?' he asked.

'Not much, sir, though the killing has shocked the whole town,' Abbot replied. 'There's still no trace of Alfred Yorke. He must have left the district. But he's a mild man. He's never been known to hurt or threaten anyone, and the general impression – for such as it's worth – is that he certainly didn't kill Le Merle.'

50

'We still need to talk to him,' Tansey said. 'He's got to be found.'

'Yes, indeed.' Abbot was silent for a minute, then he said: 'You saw today's *Courier*, sir? Spenser's report – and especially his comments – have caused a stir.'

'That young man needs his bottom smacked.'

Abbot grinned. 'I dare say Brigadier Wessex would be happy to oblige. Spenser made a lot of the fact that the Brig was known to have had a row with Le Merle and that he should have been at the Crosses' party for the new gynaecologist, Lance Ritchie, and his wife, and not anywhere near the church. Nothing actually libellous, of course, but the story's resulted in some nasty gossip. The brigadier can be very autocratic when he likes and it hasn't made him over-popular.'

'Unfortunately this kind of happening rarely brings out the best in people,' Tansey said. 'Anything else?'

'Not really, sir, though I gathered from a pal of mine who works as a senior porter at the hospital that this Mr Ritchie isn't making himself over-popular either. He gives the impression that he's really too good for poor old Colombury General, and that it's jolly kind of him to have come here.'

'Oh dear,' said Tansey. 'Where was he before?'

'One of the big teaching hospitals in London. St Mary's, I believe. But, according to my chum, they were cutting down on consultant staff and he needed a new job. Not that we weren't lucky to get him. He has a fine reputation, I gather.'

Tansey nodded. He wasn't interested in Ritchie, and they were now on the outskirts of Little Chipping, a long, straggling village of no great charm. Abbot asked the way to Lavender Cottage and after a couple of blank disclaimers he tackled a small boy who said, 'You mean that shack where old man Sutton and his missus live?' and gave directions.

The house was not a shack, but nor did it do justice to the name of Lavender Cottage. It had an unloved, uncared-for appearance. There were slates missing from the roof, the paint on the woodwork was peeling and the curtains were noticeably dirty. A mangy-looking dog, tied to a stake driven into the ground, barked madly at their approach. Abbot banged on the door; there was no bell.

The woman who opened the door was a surprise to both of them. Tansey had expected a middle-aged, downtrodden, pathetic little woman, Whitelaw a fierce, elderly harridan. Belle Sutton fulfilled neither expectation. She was about thirty, a bottle blonde with a small, sharp face, a scarlet mouth and false eyelashes; her teeth, when she smiled, were yellow from tobacco.

Tansey introduced himself and Abbot, and Mrs Sutton showed them into the front room. A querulous voice called from upstairs, asking who the visitors were, and Belle shouted, 'Police!'

'He'll be down in a mo,' she said.

It was a long moment while they listened to the creaking of the stairs and heard Bill Sutton's harsh breathing. He was a small man, twice as old as his wife, and he showed his age. Without greeting the police officers he collapsed into an armchair.

'Emphysema,' he said when at last he managed to speak. 'It's going to kill me before long.'

'Nonsense, Dad,' his wife said. 'You're going to live to a ripe old age.'

'We're sorry to bother you, sir, but we're making inquiries about Father Le Merle's death, and you may be able to help us,' Tansey said. 'Perhaps Mrs Sutton could answer our questions to save you the trouble, sir. It's about Saturday evening. We believe Father Hanson visited you.'

'Dad had one of his turns and I sent for the priest,' Mrs Sutton said.

'The priest? Not a doctor?' Abbot spoke involuntarily.

'Dad always thinks he's going to die, and a priest is more use than old Dr Hobson, who does him no good anyway.'

'That's the girl's idea,' Sutton said. 'It's my belief the priest comes to see her, not me.'

Tansey thought of the lipstick on Hanson's collar, but he made no comment. 'It's a question of timing,' he said. 'If we're certain about Father Hanson's times we can check other people by him.'

'Why don't you ask him, then,' Sutton wheezed.

'We did, but his statement has to be confirmed.' Tansey hurried on. 'What time did he arrive here on Saturday?'

'Soon after half past four,' Belle Sutton said, 'and he went straight upstairs to Dad.'

'He sat and talked for ten minutes or so and mumbled a prayer. I was wishing him gone,' Sutton said. 'It was hard enough to breathe, without him gawping at me.'

'He would have left here before five then?' Tansey said.

'Ye-es.' Mrs Sutton seemed doubtful. 'I offered him a cuppa. I thought it a kind thing to do, but –' Suddenly she became purposeful. 'Sure, he left before five.'

'You heard him go, Mr Sutton?'

'I heard his car leave. He revved the engine as if he couldn't get it to start.' Sutton sounded aggrieved. 'He's not much of a driver. And the dog made a real rumpus.'

'So we can say Father Hanson was here from four-thirty to five approximately,' Tansey said. 'Thank you. That's very useful to know.'

Tansey was silent for several minutes after Abbot drove away from Lavender Cottage. He had not liked the Suttons – he had particularly distrusted Belle Sutton – but he could think of no reason why either of them should lie.

'If Hanson left here about five he should have been home long before six,' he said suddenly. 'Yet when Gough went to the presbytery to tell him about Le Merle, Hanson said he had just come in. And why was he drinking?'

Abbot said, 'You mean, it could have been him who killed Le Merle, sir?'

'It's possible. According to their housekeeper, the priests had quarrelled – quite a bitter quarrel, she said, about the old tramp – and it seems he did have the time and opportunity, if the Suttons' evidence is to be accepted.'

'And he'd need a drink or two if he had done it,' Abbot added.

Tansey laughed. 'Don't let's jump to conclusions. Did you believe what the Suttons had to say, Abbot?'

'Yes and no, sir. That is, I'd be prepared to believe the

timing, as the two of them agree on that, but I wouldn't trust the woman in general like. There was something kind of unpleasant about her.'

'I know what you mean,' Tansey said thoughtfully. 'She put me off too. But let's go and see what our Father Hanson has to say, if he's at home.'

Father Hanson was indeed at home, and opened the door himself with a welcoming smile which faded when he saw who his visitors were. 'Not now!' he said. 'Not now!' And for a split second Tansey thought he was going to shut the door in their faces.

'Father Hanson, we need to have a word with you,' Tansey said. 'It shouldn't take long if you're expecting someone.'

'Yes, I am. Father Sinclair. He should be here now. The bishop has arranged for him to fill in until a permanent arrangement can be made. There's too much work in the parish for one priest.'

'Sure, I understand,' Tansey said. 'But this will only take a moment. If we might come in –'

They were still standing on the doorstep of the presbytery, and reluctantly Hanson let them into the hall. But he made no attempt to show them into the parlour.

Annoyed, Tansey said, 'Father Hanson, do I have to remind you that this is a murder inquiry? The police have the right to expect the truth from witnesses – the whole truth. We have just been to see Mr and Mrs Sutton at Lavender Cottage.'

'You won't get the truth from her!' Hanson burst out. 'She – she makes things up. She's a – a bad woman.'

'I'm not interested in Mrs Sutton's morals – if that's what you're hinting at – or yours either, Father Hanson.' Tansey emphasized the word 'Father'. 'The Suttons, both of them, agree that on Saturday evening you left Lavender Cottage no later than five, but you claim to have arrived back here at the presbytery around six at the earliest. How do you account for the discrepancy?'

'I . . . I . . .' Father Hanson's face seemed to be turning red and white by turns. 'I had a puncture. I had to change the tyre. It took me some time. I'm not very good at –'

Tansey cut him short. 'Thank you, Father Hanson.' He exchanged glances with Abbot, making it clear that he had not believed Hanson. 'We'll say goodbye then – for now.'

CHAPTER 6

Cyril Bristow described himself as a jobbing gardener. Weather permitting, he worked some six hours a day, five days a week. At the weekends he tended his own small plot, played snooker, had a pint or two at the local, and went to chapel with his wife. It was a pleasant life. Had he wished, he could have had twice as much work – many of the houses around Colombury had large gardens – but he was getting on for sixty, his children had long since left home, and he saw no reason to do more.

On the Tuesday after Father Le Merle's death, Cyril Bristow went as usual to the home of Mr and Mrs Pettigrew, who lived next door to Brigadier and Mrs Wessex. It had rained all the previous day and overnight, so that the ground would be wet and heavy, and he nearly decided to spend the morning in bed, especially as he had the beginnings of a cold. But if he didn't go he wouldn't be paid, and because of the weather he had missed a great deal of work lately. Besides there would surely be something he would be able to do, sweeping up leaves, or in the greenhouse.

He arrived at the Pettigrews' house at nine o'clock. The sun was breaking through a watery sky, and Bristow felt more cheerful. The wind and the rain over the weekend had brought down a lot of leaves and small branches and, collecting his wheelbarrow, he set to work to take pile after pile to the compost heap. He was proud of his compost.

He was working away under the wall at the far end of the garden, and thinking that it would soon be time for him to go along to the kitchen for his mug of coffee, when he saw something glinting among the leaves. He swept it towards him and picked it up. Like everyone in the district he read the *Courier*, and he had heard both the official news and much gossip about Father Le Merle's death. He knew at once what he was holding, the historic St Stephen's chalice, though it looked like no more than a tarnished silver cup.

His first thought when he had recovered from his initial surprise was that there might be a reward, but he was not a mercenary man and he dismissed the idea. He couldn't take a reward for restoring stolen property to a church. He plodded up to the house.

'You're early for coffee this morning, Cyril,' said Olga Pettigrew, who was busy baking cakes for a bazaar which one of her pet charities was about to hold. 'Cold outside, is it?'

'No, it's not that, ma'am. I've found that cup thing what was stolen from St Stephen's at the far end of the garden. 'Twas lucky I didn't put it on my compost heap. It was just lying among the leaves and stuff.'

Mrs Pettigrew was a practical woman. She fetched the *Courier* and telephoned the number given there – that of the incident van behind the police station – which was to be called if anyone had information concerning Father Le Merle's death or the stolen chalice. She didn't need to compare the object Bristow had found with the description in the newspaper. How it had come to be in her garden was a mystery, but there was no doubt about its identity.

She was assured that someone would be at her house within half an hour. The someone turned out to be Inspector Whitelaw, who realized that the house was next dooor to that of Brigadier Wessex, and that the large gardens abutted. He found Mrs Pettigrew having coffee and staring in bemused awe at the chalice which sat in all its splendour on the kitchen table. Cyril had polished it before Mrs Pettigrew had been able to prevent him. Whitelaw was offered a cup of coffee, which he accepted gratefully.

'I'd like to see where you found this object, Mr Bristow,' Whitelaw said.

'I'll show you, sir. The exact spot. It were at the far end of the garden, by the wall.'

'There's a road just outside the wall, isn't there? How high is the wall?'

'About six feet,' Mrs Pettigrew answered. 'You think someone threw it over, Inspector?'

'It would seem to me very likely.'

'But why steal it and then throw it away?' Mrs Pettigrew shook her head in puzzlement. 'And why choose our garden? I suppose that could have been chance, but I rather wish he'd chosen somewhere else. We'll have reporters and cameras all over the place once they learn about it, which won't please my husband in the least. He likes his privacy.'

'I'm afraid you'll have the police first, in force,' Whitelaw said. 'Your garden and those of your neighbours, not to mention the verge outside the wall, will all have to be subjected to a thorough search.'

'But you've got the chalice.' Mrs Pettigrew stopped abruptly. 'Sorry. I'm being stupid. I suppose he might have left clues.'

'Possibly. It's wonderful what the forensic boys can do these days. And we haven't found the weapon yet.'

'You think he might have thrown the knife into our garden too? What an unpleasant idea.'

Whitelaw nearly said that murder was necessarily unpleasant, but he knew what a shock even a distant contact with violent crime can be to someone who has never experienced it before and who has imagination. The phlegmatic Bristow, who had actually found the chalice, was far less affected.

'I didn't see no knife, Inspector,' he said. 'Mind you, I didn't look. I wish I had. But I did find the chalice!'

He was triumphant, and Whitelaw had a mental picture of the old gardener holding forth in his local pub to an enthralled audience; finding the chalice could be one of the big events of his life. He hadn't seen Father Le Merle's body, and it hadn't occurred to him that the killer might kill again.

Whitelaw swallowed his own feelings of unease and smiled

at them both. 'Well, if you'll show me the exact spot where you found the chalice, Mr Bristow, I'll lay on the search. And with luck it should be over long before Mr Pettigrew comes home.'

This proved to be true, but it took the best part of the day and a great number of police hours were consumed, unfortunately without result. The knife was not found. Nor was there any lead to explain why the chalice should have been thrown away or by whom, a fact that didn't surprise Inspector Whitelaw who, having organized the search, had left it to Sergeant Donaldson and his men. However, one thing seemed quite clear. Brigadier Wessex wouldn't have been so stupid as to throw the chalice into the garden of his immediate neighbours.

Francis Sinclair, Father Sinclair, had been grieved to hear of Father Le Merle's death. Not only were they fellow priests, but they had also received their training at the English College in Rome. Moreover, because they were both much of an age, they had naturally tended to seek each other's company, and had become friends. Over the years, however, they had inevitably drifted apart and their friendship was by now reduced to letters at Christmas and Easter, and rare meetings. Father Sinclair thought sadly of the past and all that might have been.

He was a man of above medium height, who liked to wear breeches and boots, and this, together with his dark hair and beard, gave an impression of virility and physical strength, which at the present time was somewhat misleading. Father Sinclair had recently had a serious heart operation from which he was recovering slowly, and which meant that he had been free to 'help out' Father Hanson.

He had not been impressed by the young Father Hanson, who, in his opinion, was not coping well with an admittedly difficult situation. Hanson gave the impression of being extremely nervous, of being unsure of what he was saying so that he contradicted himself, of having some kind of phobia about the police. He did not seem likely to prove a very satisfactory colleague.

'That will be Superintendent Tansey,' Hanson said when the doorbell rang. 'I knew he'd be back, though I can't imagine what more I can tell him.'

The two priests were considering the division of their labours until the time a permanent replacement for Father Le Merle could be found. Sinclair would have been happy merely to assume the dead priest's duties; it appeared to him the simplest arrangement, but it was apparent that Hanson was eager to be rid of some of the visits to the sick in the outlying villages. As Sinclair was not familiar with the district it seemed to him absurd that he should take over this task, and he was glad of the interruption which stilled the too vehement protests he might have made.

For his part, Hanson, though not pleased at the prospect of any visit from the police, was thankful that the visitor was not Superintendent Tansey but Inspector Whitelaw by himself, without that sergeant who said little but took copious notes. Moreover, Whitelaw had come to return the chalice. Both the priests were delighted, though Father Sinclair's delight was tempered by doubts.

'Won't you need the chalice as evidence, Inspector? I assume it was taken by Father Le Merle's murderer.'

'That's a fair assumption, sir, but what with the treatment it has received from the weather and the handling it's had, I'm afraid it's no use to us in that respect at the moment. We've taken a statement from the man who found it, and I would like a receipt from you. Meanwhile, we thought it best in your care.'

Whitelaw rose to go, and Hanson was happy to see him out, but at the front door the inspector turned to him. 'We should like you to come to Thames Valley Police headquarters in Kidlington at ten o'clock tomorrow morning, Father Hanson. Ask for me. Is that convenient?'

'Con-convenient, yes. But why?'

'We require you to make a formal statement about your movements on the evening of Saturday last, and I would suggest you give the matter some thought, before you swear to it.'

'I've already told you what –'

'Father Hanson, the four tyres of your car are equally worn. The spare is new. There's no suggestion that you had a puncture and had to change a wheel on your way back from Lavender Cottage. There is, however, more than a suggestion that, by the time you were told of Father Le Merle's death and were asked to go to the church, you were somewhat inebriated.'

'I – I don't know what you mean.'

'As I said, think about it, Father. Goodbye to you.'

Superintendent Tansey had spent the morning at head-quarters. He had had an unhappy hour with St John Cowan, the Chief Constable, who had decided that Yorke was the most likely suspect, and refused to understand that the tramp had simply disappeared.

'Someone is sheltering him, Superintendent. That's my opinion. One of those lady do-gooders who do more harm than good.'

'Yes, sir,' Tansey said politely. Holy Cow was obviously pleased with what he seemed to consider was a clever sound bite, and there was no point in suggesting he might be wrong. 'We'll find him before long,' Tansey went on. He spoke with an assurance he didn't feel and dared to glance at his watch. 'Sir, I'm very sorry, but I'm due at a press conference in a few minutes. As you know, Father Le Merle's murder has become country-wide front-page news, and we have to pla-cate the media.'

'Sure! Sure!' Cowan said. Suddenly he gave one of his unexpected grins, which made Tansey sometimes like him. 'Perhaps you'd better not mention my comment about the lady do-gooders to the press. My wife might not take it too well.'

'No, of course not, sir. I understand,' Tansey said. 'I'll be tactful.'

And how necessary tact was, Dick Tansey thought as later he sat in a corner of the officers' mess at headquarters, eating a solitary lunch. There was an art in dealing with the media, and it was one he had never really mastered. He had little difficulty in making a statement. It was the questions that followed which could prove a minefield. A direct question that for some reason he didn't wish to answer had to be sidestepped; a blank refusal too often led to intensive probing. Another query, seemingly innocuous, could be the forerunner of an unanswerable question containing a hidden smear or innuendo. And there was always the chance of misinterpretation, either accidental or deliberate.

This morning's press conference had been no different from any other. The known facts were few. Father Le Merle was extremely well liked in the community, and there seemed to be no reason for his murder, other than the possibility that he had interrupted a thief who had first forced him to open the safe and then killed him.

But there had been a few difficult questions. Someone asked if Father Le Merle and Father Hanson got on well together, and followed this with an irrelevant question about whether the murderer might have been a drunk who had wandered into the church. Someone else wanted to know why Brigadier Wessex had been prepared to arrive late at the party given by Mr and Mrs Bernard Cross in honour of Mr and Mrs Lance Ritchie; surely at best it had been discourteous. Tansey had waved this away and concentrated on other questions about the nurses and the down-and-out Alfred Yorke.

Tansey was thankful when the press conference was over. It had not been one of the easiest, although it was so early in the case that the media could hardly expect substantive answers. But they had been there in force, and for this he blamed the *Courier*. He guessed that Tim Spenser, knowing he couldn't confine the story to his own paper, had sold his version to the national daily for which he was a stringer – not for money, but because a favour given was a favour to be returned – and the tabloids had caught on. The hounds had smelt blood, perhaps a nice juicy scandal involving the Roman Catholic Church, which was welcome in a week when news was scarce.

Cursing Spenser, the superintendent finished a cup of coffee that he had allowed to grow cold and was almost undrinkable. He was not looking forward to the afternoon.

He hated postmortems. He had never got used to them and Dr Ghent, brilliant pathologist though he most certainly was, was also an unpredictable individual who was helpful or unhelpful as the mood took him.

This particular Tuesday afternoon proved to be even worse than Tansey had anticipated. The superintendent was not personally a religious man and he had not known Father Le Merle, but Ghent's flamboyant treatment of the priest's intestines revolted him. He tried to think of other things while Ghent, cheerfully muttering his findings to his assistants, continued his exploration, but the strong smell of formaldehyde made him constantly aware of where he was and what was happening to the dead priest's body.

He was more thankful than usual when the autopsy was over and they had retreated to the pathologist's office where, as a contrast to the distressing associations of the operating theatre, afternoon tea was served by Ghent's secretary; the teapot was not silver, but the china was bone, the tea Earl Grey, the biscuits from Fortnums. It always surprised Tansey how Ghent, so fastidious in every other way, had no respect for persons once they were dead.

'Well, I can tell you something right now, Superintendent,' Ghent said. Although he and Tansey had known each other for several years they always addressed each other formally. 'Le Merle died as a result of a knife wound.'

'So I assumed,' Tansey said, trying not to sound sarcastic.

'Ah, Superintendent, you didn't listen to what I said. I said *a* knife wound. That should tell you quite a lot about the killer.'

'Are you implying that he didn't *intend* to kill, that Le Merle's death was accidental?'

'That is a possibility, but I rather think not. I would say that the killer was a cool, calculating character. We know he wore gloves and had armed himself with a knife – not unusual even among minor villains these days, as you are only too well aware, Superintendent. But he struck this one fatal blow, then wiped the bloody knife on the priest's soutane, as we can tell from the stains; my report will make that clear. He made no attempt to strike again. There was no sign of frenzy about his attack.'

'Murder with intent,' Tansey murmured. 'But why? I've never favoured the interrupted thief theory, if only because the body was in the wrong position. Incidentally, the chalice has been found, thrown over a garden wall. But why should anyone want to kill a priest whom everyone seemed to admire?'

'Maybe the killer had confessed to some ghastly crime and then had second thoughts, was scared the good priest might blab his nasty secret.' Ghent laughed.

'I doubt it,' Tansey said, and, taking advantage of Ghent's good humour, asked, 'Any more?'

To his surprise, Ghent nodded with great seriousness. 'Yes. Either it was a very lucky blow – in which case why didn't he strike again to make sure? – or he knew exactly what he was doing. He knew the knife thrust would pierce the correct artery, causing the lungs to flood with blood so that death would be almost instantaneous.'

'You mean –'

'Yes, the killer had medical knowledge. He could have been a nurse –'

'Could it have been a woman?' Tansey interrupted.

'Possibly. The blow was struck downwards, so she would have to be at least as tall as Le Merle, but the priest wasn't a big man. However, she – or whoever it was – must have had serious medical training. I emphasize that in my report, which you'll get tomorrow.'

'In the meantime, very many thanks,' Tansey said.

He was indeed grateful. He was no nearer knowing or even suspecting who the killer might be, but Ghent had provided evidence that could be invaluable.

CHAPTER 7

'Good morning, Superintendent Tansey.'

The voice was educated, cultivated, controlled. It did not fit the man who, at a gesture from Tansey, had seated himself across the desk in the superintendent's office. And the slight smile, not quite contemptuous, in the circumstances showed surprising self-confidence. The visitor crossed one leg over the other, revealing under a filthy raincoat a long tear in his trouser leg, but this didn't seem to disconcert him.

'Your name is Alfred Yorke?'

'That is so.'

'Where do you live, Mr Yorke?'

'No fixed abode.' Yorke grinned and Tansey noted that his teeth were good. 'St Stephen's church usually finds me.'

'Do I put that down under address, sir?' asked Abbot, who was sitting to one side, taking notes.

'No, don't bother, Sergeant.'

Tansey regarded Alfred Yorke coldly. He was beginning to understand why Yorke irritated Brigadier Wessex so much. This man with his old clothes, his long dirty hair, his bitten nails and the smell of refuse that he seemed to exude, nevertheless had a certain distinction which was difficult to define. Tansey warned himself not to let Yorke rile him.

'Mr Yorke, you were in St Stephen's church last Saturday evening. I see you wear a watch. What time did you go into the church?' he asked.

'Around half past four. Mrs Faudin, the priest's house-keeper, had given me a cup of tea. She's a kind lady.'

'And you didn't leave the church until –'

'Until the fuss started.'

Tansey said, 'Mr Yorke, Father Le Merle was killed

between four and six o'clock, at which time on your own admission you were in the church. What do you say to that?'

'Not guilty.' Yorke showed no sign of concern. 'As soon as I got there I stretched out on my pew and had a good kip. I was tired. I woke about an hour later, about half past five. I sneezed in my sleep and that woke me. I decided I'd better have something to eat before Mass – I had a few sandwiches with me and I opened them out in the pew.'

'And you saw no one, heard no one?'

'I saw no one. I heard someone shuffling around. As soon as I was properly awake I started to have my supper. Then the lights came on. I saw the old Misses Blair had made it up the aisle to their pew, and the brigadier, who was glaring at me, as usual. After that there was a certain amount of confusion while the brigadier investigated the sacristy, and eventually emerged and announced that there would be no Mass that evening. I sensed there was going to be some kind of trouble – perhaps Father Le Merle had had a serious accident – and it seems I was right. Anyway, I didn't intend to wait for it. Perhaps the police would get involved, and I'd have another brush with that Sergeant Donaldson. So I made my way quietly out of the church. I think that's all I can tell you – about me or anyone else.'

Tansey's questions continued for another ten minutes, but to no avail. Alfred Yorke stuck firmly to his story. Asked why he hadn't come forward before, he said he had been living in the woods and didn't know he was wanted. But his voice had become harsh and he seemed to have difficulty in breathing. At a nod from Tansey, Abbot went to find him a tumbler of water which he drank thirstily.

'Thanks,' he said. He had become pale and was sweating a little; in fact, he looked ill. 'I'm not feeling my best. I think I may be getting a touch of flu.'

Tansey nodded; reluctantly he felt sorry for the man. 'Okay, Mr Yorke. Sergeant Abbot will have your statement typed and get you to read and sign it. When you've done that, you can go. If I were you, I'd get along to the hospital and have someone look at you.'

'I can go?' Yorke was on his feet, as if he feared the superintendent might change his mind. 'Right. Good morning to you then, Superintendent.'

'Good morning,' Tansey said, and as he watched the door of his office close behind Yorke and Sergeant Abbot, he hoped he hadn't made a mistake.

Dick Tansey found himself staring fixedly at the tumbler from which Alfred Yorke had drunk the water Abbot had procured for him. Yorke had seized the tumbler like an innocent man, eager to quench his thirst – or like a man so in need of liquid that it had caused him to disregard any other thought. Either way he would have left an excellent set of fingerprints on the glass.

Tansey produced a small plastic bag from his desk, carefully put the glass inside and labelled it. Possibly this was a waste of time, but it would be interesting to see if the computer bank of prints at the Yard came up with anything on Alfred Yorke. Certainly he needed to know considerably more about Yorke, if for no other reason than that the man had lied.

The weather had been atrocious for most of the time since the beginning of the week and if, as he said, Yorke had been sleeping rough in the woods, he would have been much dirtier than he was. For instance, Tansey could have sworn that his hair had been recently washed and, although there was a certain unpleasant smell from his clothes, he did not stink as Tansey had been led to believe, and his body, even in a warm office, did not give off that sour odour that was so offensive to others.

Tansey guessed that Yorke had spent the last few days in some sort of refuge for down-and-outs, where he had been forced to wash. Why he hadn't been prepared to admit to this was a mystery. It could scarcely be a matter of pride. Pride and Alfred Yorke were not compatible.

The superintendent's thoughts were interrupted by the telephone. A knife, very probably the knife that had taken Father Le Merle's life, had been found in a drain at the top of the lane beside St Stephen's church. It was long-handled, extremely sharp and would have been the ideal weapon for the killer. However, there was nothing distinctive about it. It might have been bought in almost any specialist or department store, so that it would be next to impossible to trace. And several days in a drain would not have helped. Nevertheless, the forensic boys would do their best.

Tansey appreciated the 'very probably'. The *Courier* would have no such doubts, and for once he agreed with the paper. It was the first and simplest place for the killer to have got rid of the knife and, if the drain hadn't been blocked by leaves and heavy overnight rain, it might not have been found, at least for some considerable time. He blamed himself; he should have thought of drains before, especially after the chalice had been found.

Thoughtfully he recalled the evidence of the youth, Jason Clark, who had been certain he had seen a tall man in a raincoat leave St Stephen's church around 5.30 the previous Saturday, and return approximately fifteen minutes later. This would have been more than adequate time for the killer to have left the church, rid himself of the knife, and returned. But Jason had been vague about times – and the description fitted Alfred Yorke.

Should he have allowed Yorke to go free? He really had no more reason to hold him than, say, Brigadier Wessex, but it was a question that was to worry him later when there was another killing.

For the moment Superintendent Tansey had forgotten about the nurse who might have been in St Stephen's, like Alfred Yorke, at the time Father Le Merle was attacked. Whoever it was who had left the church as Brigadier Wessex turned on the lights, she, or he, had not come forward, and a lot of hospital time, to the annoyance of Bernard Cross, had been wasted on fruitless interrogations of the nursing staff. Nurse Gemma Drayton, whom Inspector Whitelaw had distrusted, had not, as Tansey had hoped, volunteered any more information.

On this Wednesday morning Gemma Drayton was on duty in the private wing of the Colombury General Hospital. She was watching as Mr Ritchie, the gynaecological consultant, examined a patient and discussed with her the possibility of a Caesarean section. Gemma didn't like Ritchie much. She thought him cold and distant, and was annoyed that he seemed to have little faith in her nursing abilities; twice that morning he had asked her if she understood his instructions. But she had to admit that he was a clever and conscientious doctor, who gave patients confidence.

Now he was saying, 'I suggest you have a word with your husband. There's no immediate hurry to decide, but we mustn't leave it too long.' He smiled reassuringly at his patient.

Then from outside the room came the sound of a heavy thud as of a falling body, followed immediately by the smash of glass and the crash of metal. Gemma Drayton, who had been nearer to the door, was out first, but Ritchie was close behind her, and it was he who crouched and bent over the nurse who lay sprawled on the floor beside an overturned trolley with its scattered and broken equipment.

'I think it's just a faint,' he said as the girl opened her eyes.

'No! No! No!' she cried, pushing Ritchie away, so that he stumbled and nearly fell himself.

'It's all right, Kathy. It's me.' Gemma knelt beside her. Looking up at Ritchie, who had straightened himself, she said, 'It's Kathy Whitely.'

'Ah?' Ritchie could do no more than retreat a little; the name meant nothing to him.

By now Miss Bascombe, the ward sister, had appeared, with a small group of other people, and Miss Bascombe started to organize them. Two patients in dressing-gowns were shushed back into their rooms. A cleaner picked up the trolley and with the help of a couple of nurses began to clear up the bits and pieces of equipment on the floor. Kathy was on her feet, supported on one side by Gemma and on the other by a junior doctor, Peter Quentin, who obviously enjoyed having his arm around her.

'I'm so sorry,' Kathy said. She looked fearfully from Mr Ritchie to Sister Bascombe. 'I must have fainted. Silly of me.'

'Go and sit in the nurses' room,' Sister Bascombe ordered. She turned to Ritchie and shook her head. 'These girls! They starve themselves in order to stay slim, and then they're surprised when they faint. I'm sorry she was so ungracious to you when you were trying to help her, Mr Ritchie. I hope she didn't hurt you at all.'

'Heavens no!' Lance Ritchie laughed. 'But I doubt if slimming is her problem, Sister. She looked healthy enough to me.' He made no effort to lower his voice. 'Of course I'm not sure, but I rather think she's pregnant and was afraid I'd give away her secret.'

'Oh dear!' Sister Bascombe was angry. 'Why can't these girls be more careful? I'll have to have a word with her.'

Lance Ritchie grinned sardonically. His own wife hadn't been careful. He had been an up-and-coming registrar, with the promise of a brilliant career ahead; she had been a hospital almoner – a job until she married – and she had been determined to marry him.

She must regret it now, he thought, as he went along to his next patient. She had taken an instant dislike to Colombury and what she called its 'cottage hospital' and 'cottage-hospital mentality'. But the London hospital where he had been working had been forced to cut staff; he had to admit that perhaps he had never really fulfilled his promise and was dispensable. He had been lucky to get this job in Colombury and, come what may, he intended to keep it.

At about the same time, Father John Hanson was sitting opposite Inspector Whitelaw in an interview room at the headquarters of the Thames Valley Police. At a side table a uniformed police constable sat, notebook in front of him.

Father Hanson shivered. Unlike Alfred Yorke he was extremely nervous. He glanced at the police constable. 'Does he have to be here?' he asked.

'Yes,' Whitelaw said. 'Your statement will be typed. You will be able to read it, and then you will be required to sign it when you are satisfied that it agrees with what you wished to say.'

'But – but what about my privacy?' Hanson blustered.

'Perhaps if you had told us the truth to start with, Father, there wouldn't be this difficulty,' Whitelaw said.

70

'I – I couldn't. I can't!' The priest literally wrung his hands. 'If my bishop hears about this – if it gets in the newspapers . . . Father Le Merle was wrong. He always thought the best of people, and he wouldn't listen to me.'

Hanson was becoming hysterical and Whitelaw felt sorry for him. But the priest had hinted, however vaguely, at a possible motive for wanting to be rid of Le Merle. He couldn't be allowed to leave it at that.

'All right,' Whitelaw said. 'Go and get yourself a cup of tea, Constable. Ten minutes. And bring some back with you for us.'

'Very good, sir.' The constable went, slightly regretful not to know what the scandal was. 'Tea in ten minutes.'

'Now,' said Whitelaw, 'tell me your story, Father Hanson. I promise you if it's not connected with Father Le Merle's death, I'll treat it as a confidence, but I must have the truth.'

'It's Mrs Sutton, the woman at Lavender Cottage, near Little Chipping,' Hanson burst out. 'She pretends she's fallen in love with me. It's not true. All she wants is sex. She says her husband is past it. She keeps on sending for me on the excuse that he's about to die, but I've already given him the last rites. I tried to explain to Father Le Merle, but he didn't or he wouldn't understand. He seemed to think it was up to me to control the situation, and last Saturday – I'll never, never go near that place again.'

'Father Hanson, what happened last Saturday?' Whitelaw was getting impatient, suspecting that the priest was being over-conscientious about some petty matter. 'The constable will be back in a minute.'

'She – she flung herself at me. She caught me off balance and we fell to the ground together. She was all over me, pulling my hand up her skirt. She hadn't any knickers on and she – she unzipped my trousers. She was saying things – things I don't want to remember.' Hanson shuddered. 'Somehow I managed to push her off me and get to my feet. She was furious. She screamed that she'd tell the bishop, everyone, that I'd tried to rape her, though God knows it wasn't true. But when I was halfway home I realized my

71

trousers were still unzipped, and they – they were wet around there.'

'You didn't have actual intercourse with her?'

'Good God, no!'

Whitelaw looked at the young priest with amused despair; he had no wish to be a father confessor. 'All right,' he said. 'As far as I can see none of this has any real relevance to Father Le Merle's murder. You said you tried to explain to him, but I doubt that, if you had been as frank with him as you have with me, he'd have wished you to visit the Suttons again. If you want my advice, I think you should confide in your new priest, Father Sinclair. At least you can give him an abridged version. As for the woman, if you have any more trouble from her, which you probably won't, refer it to me, and I'll arrange for her to have an official warning.'

'You mean none of this need be in my statement? It won't be made public, get into the press?' Hanson couldn't believe his good fortune.

'That's right,' Whitelaw said as there was a knock on the door and the constable came in, carrying a tray with two mugs of tea and a bowl of sugar.

Kathy Whitely lay in bed, her hands clasped behind her head. She cursed Lance Ritchie. What right had he to tell Sister Bascombe so publicly that he thought she was pregnant? It was nothing to do with him. She had scarcely exchanged a dozen words with the man in the short time he had been at the hospital.

Gemma had said that she had pushed him roughly away and she had a vague memory of that. But she had just been regaining consciousness; she hadn't realized where she was or what she was doing, and for a fleeting moment she had been aware of that peculiar smell that had haunted her in the last few days. Ritchie should have realized that she wasn't responsible for her action, and not been so mean as to tell Sister Bascombe what he suspected.

Now the news of her pregnancy would be all around the hospital, and doubtless it would be all around Colombury. At least Brian wouldn't be able to vacillate any more. He would have to tell his mother that he wanted to marry her, if he did. Heaven knows how Mrs Minton would react. And what of her own parents? She was beset by questions. Did she really want to marry Brian Minton? Wouldn't she prefer to become Mrs Steve Poole? Too late for that now, wasn't it?

Once again she silently cursed Lance Ritchie.

CHAPTER 8

Christopher Le Merle, elder brother of Father Paul Le Merle, arrived in Oxford on Thursday morning. He checked in at the Randolph Hotel, washed his face in cold water to brighten himself, looked enviously at the bed and went downstairs. He caught a taxi to Kidlington and the headquarters of the Thames Valley Police. In the taxi he closed his eyes and dozed. He felt incredibly tired.

Christopher Le Merle was in his fifties. Married, with three children, he had lived in Jersey in the Channel Islands almost all his life, but he had travelled widely and, as one of the most successful lawyers on the island, he was a rich man. He had always been very fond of his brother, and grief at his death had been exacerbated by the manner of it.

He had been working hard and was badly in need of a rest, so he and his wife had taken a short holiday in France, and they were near Toulouse when they got the news of his brother's murder. The long drive to the ferry at St Malo, a rough sea-crossing home to Jersey, where he had left his wife and car and, after a sleepless night, an early flight to Heathrow and a bus and train journey to Oxford, had left him exhausted.

'Here we are, mister! Police headquarters, as required.'

The taxi driver caused Chris Le Merle to wake with a start. He quickly shook his head and felt for his wallet to pay the fare. He told himself that when he met Detective Superintendent Tansey he mustn't appear too dumb. But he knew so little about his brother's life.

Tansey stood up when Christopher Le Merle was shown into his office and offered his hand. 'My condolences on your brother's death, Mr Le Merle. I didn't know Father Le Merle

74

personally, but I gather he'll be greatly missed by many people in Colombury.'

'Thank you.' Le Merle sat in the chair to which Tansey pointed, but shook his head at the offer of coffee; he had drunk too much coffee in the last thirty-six hours. 'Superintendent, as you are aware, I've been in France and I know only the basic facts of what happened. Could you give me some details?'

'Your brother was killed last Saturday evening, Mr Le Merle, by a single knife thrust. He was in the sacristy of his church, St Stephen's. According to the pathologist, death was all but instantaneous, and I hope it is a consolation to you and your family that he can't have suffered.'

'Yes, that's good. But who –? Have you any idea yet, Superintendent?

'Not really, I regret to say, sir.'

Tansey went on to provide more information about the circumstances surrounding the crime, and the investigation that had so far taken place. It was nearly all in the public domain. He did not mention that the killer had probably had medical knowledge; the police had decided to keep this item to themselves.

Le Merle listened attentively. An astute lawyer, he realized that Tansey wasn't telling him everything that was known, but he didn't mind. He studied Tansey as the superintendent continued to speak. Superintendent Richard Tansey, he thought, knew his job and almost certainly did it well.

'And that's all I can tell you at present,' Tansey concluded. 'Now it's your turn, Mr Le Merle.'

'My turn?' The lawyer was surprised. 'I don't see how I can help. I haven't seen my brother for about a year, when he spent his annual holiday with us as he usually did.'

'I have seen a copy of Father Le Merle's birth certificate, so I know how old he was, that he was born in Jersey and his father was a lawyer, like you. But that's about all I know. Where did he go to school, how big was his family, did he always want to be a priest, what sort of person was he?' Tansey spoke slowly, choosing his words; he wanted Le Merle to talk about his brother, but he didn't want to prompt him. 'The more I learn about the victim, the more I hope to learn about his assassin.'

'Yes, I can appreciate that,' the lawyer said. 'That must mean that you've ruled out a chance thief – a vagrant who could be miles away by now?'

Tansey thought of Alfred Yorke, but somehow Yorke didn't fit that description. 'I never rule out a possibility, sir, but in this case I believe what you suggest to be unlikely.'

'Okay, Superintendent, I'll take your word for it.' Le Merle smiled wearily and smothered a yawn. 'But, if I'm to satisfy your questions, may I change my mind about that coffee? I haven't had much sleep lately, and the lack's caught up with me.'

'Of course,' Tansey said at once. 'You've had breakfast?'

'On the plane, thanks.'

Tansey ordered the coffee and Christopher Le Merle started to talk about his brother. Paul Le Merle had been two years younger than Christopher and they had an elder sister. Because they were so close in age, the two boys had done everything together. When they were not at school – they were weekly boarders at Victoria College – they swam and sailed, played all kinds of sports and enjoyed plays and concerts and cinemas and parties, always together.

'It was a very happy, carefree life,' Christopher Le Merle said, a trace of distress creeping into his voice. 'It came to an end when I was eighteen and Paul sixteen.'

He paused. The coffee had arrived, and Tansey poured it. Le Merle took it black and was thankful that, surprisingly, it was good and strong.

'What happened when you were eighteen?' Tansey asked.

Le Merle sighed. 'Inevitably I left school. I had always intended to go into the law firm in St Helier which my grandfather had founded, and of which my father was the senior partner. I read law at Oxford. Paul should have come up at the beginning of my third year, but he had not been well, and by the time he arrived at Oxford I was at Caen University. You probably don't know, but at that time it was essential for anyone hoping to be a Jersey advocate – the equivalent of a barrister – to study Norman law. The point of all this,

Superintendent, is that Paul and I grew apart, and we never resumed our really close relationship, though we continued to be good friends, seeing each other occasionally, as I said.'

Christopher Le Merle grew silent, lost in his thoughts. Oxford had changed Paul. For a couple of years he had worked hard and played hard, and been his usual happy self. Then he had thrown up everything, decided to go down, and had bummed around Europe and the Far East, sending his family the occasional postcard.

'He gave no explanation for his behaviour?' Tansey asked.

'Not at the time. Later, some while after he had become a priest, he told me there had been a girl whom he had loved very much. She had died suddenly, and nothing had seemed worthwhile. He couldn't stay in Oxford, constantly imagining he was seeing her across the street, and he no longer cared about his career.'

'He had intended to become a lawyer too?'

'Oh no! Paul was a medical student. For as long as I can remember he wanted to be a doctor.'

'A doctor!' Tansey heard himself repeat stupidly, and himself failed to understand how Paul Le Merle's career plans could be significant.

Le Merle appeared not to notice any oddity in the exclamation. 'I think Paul must have been a little emotionally mad for a while, but he recovered. Anyway, he came home. He worked in the office, but the law had never appealed to him. Then one day he told us he proposed to become a priest. It was the right decision for him, and I believe he had a happy life.'

'Do you know anything about the girl? How she died exactly? If they were to be married?' Tansey enquired.

'I really can't imagine that she has anything to do with this. I did meet her once, in Oxford, but I can't even remember her name. I remember I got the impression she hadn't necessarily been in love with him,' Le Merle said. 'Anyway, I'm sure they weren't formally engaged. Otherwise the family would have known. As for how she died, I've no idea.'

Tansey opened his desk drawer and took out an envelope

containing a copy of the photograph that Abbot had found in one of the priest's books. He passed it to Le Merle. 'Your brother kept this snapshot – it was among his few personal possessions – so he must have treasured it.'

Le Merle looked at the photograph. 'That's her,' he said sadly. 'A pretty girl with an intelligent face. May I have this print?'

'In due course, sir. It's evidence,' Tansey said, a little mendaciously. 'As you know, there are various formalities that must be adhered to, especially as this is a murder case.'

'I understand, Superintendent. That is why I'm here,' Christopher Le Merle said. 'And to arrange to take my brother home when that's possible.'

Superintendent Tansey had said that he was not to be disturbed while Mr Le Merle was with him, so Inspector Whitelaw received the fax from London. The fingerprints on the glass tumbler from which Alfred Yorke had drunk in the superintendent's office had been put through the national computer. The findings were more than interesting.

Whitelaw was not surprised that the prints should have been on record. In his experience, characters like Yorke were apt to get into trouble with the police, small crimes such as petty theft often leading to more serious affairs such as robbery with violence. Yorke had not followed this pattern, however.

First, he was not, or had not been known previously, as Alfred Yorke. His full name was Alfred John Yorke Compton – known to his friends as 'Freddie' – and he had the courtesy title of Honourable. He had been educated at Ampleforth College and Oxford University, and had eventually been sent down without a degree. He had had a variety of jobs, mostly obtained by string-pulling, but had stuck to none of them.

One night at a nightclub, slightly drunk, he had quarrelled violently with a man in his party. He had seized a knife from the table and thrust it into the man's chest again and again. The man had died. The charge had been murder, but this was later reduced to manslaughter. The Honourable Alfred John Yorke Compton had served eight years in prison, where he had caused no trouble and got full remission for good behaviour.

Inspector Whitelaw stared at the fax. He put down the receiver and sat, contemplating its implications. Dick Tansey, he thought, was not going to be pleased about this development. If he had known that Yorke had killed a man, and killed him with a knife, he would never have allowed the man to leave headquarters. Whitelaw wondered what he should do.

Slowly he reached for the telephone. He called Colombury police station; no one there had seen or heard anything of Alfred Yorke recently. St Stephen's presbytery was equally unhelpful, though Father Hanson did go across to inspect the church in case there were signs of food or any other indication that Yorke had visited the place. Finally, Whitelaw tried the Windrush Arms, where he had been told Yorke was not infrequently given leftovers; the answer was equally negative. Since his interview with Superintendent Tansey the previous day, Alfred Yorke had once again disappeared.

'He must be found, and quickly,' Tansey said a little later when Whitelaw told him of Yorke's identification and his record. 'My mistake,' he admitted.

'But we agreed he had no motive,' Whitelaw protested. 'Father Le Merle was good to him, too good according to some people.'

'Nevertheless, we now know that Yorke is – or was – a violent man. I agree that he doesn't seem to fit the role of the priest's killer. One would have expected a sudden frenzied attack, similar to that in the club and not premeditated, the reverse of what actually happened. There's little doubt that Le Merle's killing was carefully planned and carried out in a cold-blooded – I nearly said professional – fashion. It doesn't fit. I realize that, Maurice, but we simply can't risk it. I can't risk it.' Tansey was adamant. 'We need Yorke safely on remand in prison, while inquiries continue. After all, he is a material witness, he has a record for manslaughter, and he's not a character to whom bail would be lightly given. In fact, at the moment he's gone missing. Heaven knows what the Chief Constable will say.'

'Let's hope Yorke turns up again,' Whitelaw said. 'And that we get some other leads.'

His hopes were to be fulfilled, but not in the manner that either he or Tansey would have wished.

Nurse Kathy Whitely, having fainted the previous morning in an undignified and spectacular fashion, had been grateful when Sister Bascombe sent her home to rest, and told her not to come on duty until the evening shift of the next day; they would, Sister Bascombe said, discuss her pregnancy later. But on Thursday afternoon she felt genuinely sick – it was not an excuse – and she sent a message by another nurse to say she wouldn't be able to work that evening.

As time passed, however, she felt better. A conscientious nurse, she worried about the shift, which she knew was understaffed, and finally she decided to report for duty. She showered and dressed quickly, and shortly before six set off from the nurses' home for the hospital. It was little more than a ten-minute walk, mostly through the hospital grounds. In summer this was pleasant, but as winter approached and the evenings drew in, it was not so agreeable. Nevertheless, there had never been any trouble.

One stretch of the path, along a side of the building, was particularly badly lit. The nurses had complained about this, but nothing had been done, and since they normally went along there in twos or threes or even larger groups, they hadn't made an issue of it. This evening, however, Kathy was alone.

It was dark and beginning to spit with rain. Head down, Kathy hurried, half-regretting her decision to go to the hospital. She never noticed a shadow, more solid than the rest, which detached itself from the shrubbery. But some instinct warned her. She half turned, but too late to avoid the blow to the back of her neck.

Nevertheless, she didn't completely lose consciousness. She was aware of being dragged off the path into deeper darkness and of hands touching her. The thought crossed her mind that she was going to be raped, and she tried to cry out, but the hands were now round her throat and she couldn't breathe. Within seconds she was dead.

CHAPTER 9

Friday dawned fair and bright, with a crispness in the air that made Dr Peter Quentin wish that he was off to play a round of golf, rather than facing hospital rounds. Quentin was a tall, thin, fair-haired man with a little-boy-lost look that women usually found attractive, but which was quite belied by his character. In fact, he was determined and ambitious. Not for him a country practice like his father's; one of these days he intended to become a first-class consultant in a leading hospital, together with a lucrative private practice. In the meantime he was content to work hard, to study and not to get too seriously involved with any girl.

Quentin lived in rooms in Colombury within easy walking distance of the hospital. This morning, as usual, he entered the grounds of the nurses' home and followed the path taken by Kathy Whitely the previous evening. Ahead of him were two nurses, deep in conversation, but he made no attempt to overtake them. He was content with his own company, and he wanted to watch them.

He passed the place where Kathy had been attacked, stopped, hesitated, and then turned back. He had seen a flash of red among the shrubs. The two nurses had surely seen it too, but they had ignored it. Why shouldn't he? But against his will he found himself drawn into the bushes. The red visible from the path was the lining of a nurse's cloak – Kathy Whitely's.

He gazed down on Kathy's body and felt the phlegm rise in his throat. He noted the bruise marks on her neck, the staring eyes and, to his shame, was excited by the stretch of white thigh revealed by her rucked-up clothes. He didn't

82

attempt to touch her, to feel for a pulse; he knew she was dead.

'Hello!' a voice said as Quentin returned to the path. 'What are you up to, Peter? Having a quick pee in the bushes?'

Steve Poole was not the person Quentin would have chosen to meet at that particular moment. Poole, a member of the hospital's physiotherapy team, was a former boyfriend of Kathy Whitely, and for that reason alone Quentin resented him. But he was also an extrovert – the opposite of Quentin in every way – with a mordant sense of humour.

'Nurse Whitely has been murdered, strangled, I think,' he said slowly, and he thought how stupid the formal words sounded, how meaningless.

'Kathy? You're saying Kathy's dead?' Poole ran a hand through his thick dark hair. 'If this is some kind of joke, Quentin –'

'No joke. Look for yourself.' Quentin gestured to the bushes.

Poole started forward, then stopped. 'Better not. The fuzz won't want the place trampled over in case there are clues.' He looked at Quentin oddly. 'How did you know she was there?'

Quentin didn't bother to answer. He had got over his first shock and was in control of himself. 'Go and find Cross,' he said. 'Tell him Nurse Whitely has been killed. He'll know what to do. He'll call the authorities.'

Poole hesitated. 'What about you?'

'I'll stay here until the police come. The path will have to be blocked off. Meanwhile, anyone could – could go in there.' With relief he saw Sister Bascombe approaching and knew that she would automatically take charge, and would control any over-curious nurse who was passing. 'Hurry, Poole!'

'All right! All right! I'm on my way.' Poole was still reluctant. He didn't trust Peter Quentin, not after what Kathy had told him, but then he too caught sight of Sister Bascombe and his doubts were resolved.

'Obviously she's been there all night. There's heavy dew on the body. No question of a weapon at the moment. She's been strangled. Any fool can see that from the marks on the throat. Whether strangulation was the cause of death is another matter. I'll tell you that on Monday, Superintendent.'

'Thank you,' said Tansey meekly, accepting that Dr Ghent was in one of his more uncooperative moods. He turned to Dr Porter, as Ghent, without a word of farewell, went off towards his car. 'Can you add anything to that – unofficially, Alan?'

The police surgeon grinned. 'Medically, no, but, from my knowledge of Dr Ghent, whose ability and flair I admire tremendously, I'd hazard a guess that he suspects there's something odd about this strangling.'

'That's interesting,' Tansey said. 'What makes you think it – Ghent's manner?'

'Leave it,' said Porter. 'I may be quite wrong. Let's wait and see what results Ghent comes up with on Monday.'

'Fair enough,' agreed Tansey, and together they set off towards the hospital, leaving Inspector Whitelaw to oversee the police procedures, routine in such a case.

Photographs had to be taken, the body removed and despatched to the forensic department in Oxford, and the ground over the whole area subjected to a fingertip search. The last was a lengthy business which usually produced little information of value, though there was always the off-chance of a careless footprint or a fragment of material caught on a branch. Nothing was too small to be ignored. Meanwhile, the path from the nurses' home to the hospital was sealed off, except to authorized persons, so that everyone else had to go around the long way by the road.

Bernard Cross was waiting for Tansey at the hospital entrance. The news had spread. Dr Porter said goodbye and went to collect his car; for the moment there was nothing more he could do. 'This is a most dreadful business, Superintendent, even worse from our point of view than Father Le Merle's death. I'll do anything I can to help,' Cross said.

'I appreciate that, sir,' Tansey replied. 'May we use the

room you lent us before? I'm afraid I shall have to interview quite a few of your staff.'

'Of course,' said Cross. 'Meantime, how soon will the path be open again? It's a damned nuisance having it out of bounds.'

Tansey said, 'We'll do our best, sir.' He was thinking. Kathy Whitely's death, because it was the second murder in the same week and approximately the same place, was a bitter blow to him, too. He cursed himself for having let Alfred Yorke go free. Whether or not Yorke was guilty he didn't know, but certainly he was the most likely suspect, especially if Kathy Whitely had been in St Stephen's church the previous Saturday evening. She had denied it when questioned before with all the other nurses, but –

Suddenly he realized that, while he stood there lost in thought, Cross was holding the main door open for him, and someone – Tim Spenser from the *Courier* – was calling his name. 'You go ahead, sir,' he said to Cross, and waited for Spenser to reach him.

'Good morning, Superintendent.' Although he had been running, Spenser was not in the least out of breath. 'Or perhaps it isn't a good morning for you?'

'What do you want, Mr Spenser?'

'Some gen on this latest murder, naturally, Superintendent. Do you think the Whitely girl was the nurse seen running from St Stephen's last Saturday?'

'The nurse was running down the lane beside the church, Mr Spenser. Let's be accurate.' Tansey corrected him.

'Okay, but it's a fair assumption she saw something the killer wished she hadn't, which is why he's done for her now.'

'If that were so, why did he wait several days and let her have plenty of opportunity to tell us what she knew?'

'Search me, Superintendent. It's your job to answer such questions, not mine.'

'Then perhaps you'll let me get on with it,' Tansey said coldly, turning towards the hospital door.

'You've not found Alfred Yorke yet, Superintendent?'

Dick Tansey turned back and gave Spenser's young,

innocent face a long look. It was blackmail, of course, a mild sort of blackmail, but blackmail nevertheless. They both knew it. If the superintendent refused to be helpful, the *Courier* would undoubtedly slant the news of *another* murder in Colombury so as to show the Thames Valley Police Force, and Superintendent Richard Tansey particularly, in the worst possible light. Holy Cow, the Chief Constable, would not be pleased.

Tansey decided he had no alternative but to appear co-operative. 'No, Yorke hasn't been found,' he said. 'He seems to be an elusive character. And honestly I can't tell you much about Nurse Whitely. She's been dead at least twelve hours. She was attacked on the path and pulled into the bushes where she was strangled. She was found this morning by a Dr Quentin on his way here.'

'Dr Quentin? Peter Quentin?' Spenser laughed. 'Well, that's a happy coincidence. Had the Whitely girl been assaulted?'

'Assaulted? She's dead!'

'I mean sexually assaulted.'

'Not obviously. Dr Ghent, the pathologist, didn't mention it. Nor did Dr Porter.' Tansey looked searchingly at the reporter. 'What are you trying to tell me, Spenser?'

'Only that when Kathy Whitely went out on a date with Dr Quentin one time, he tried to rape her. And him a good Catholic, too.'

When, aroused by the telephone, he had got out of bed that Friday morning, Superintendent Tansey had never heard of Kathy Whitely, but by mid-morning he knew a great deal about her.

She had been born Kathleen Patricia Whitely. She was twenty-three years old. Her parents, Colin and Gwen Whitely, lived in Little Chipping, the village not far from Colombury; Kathy had been their only child. WPC Gray and another officer would be on their way to break the unhappy news to them, and arrange for one of them to make a formal identification.

As a nurse, Kathy had been competent and reliable, but

Sister Bascombe had said, 'I don't think she had her heart in her work. She usually had an eye on the clock, if you know what I mean.'

Tansey understood; he knew police officers like that, and they rarely got promoted. Nevertheless, Sister Bascombe had added, 'But don't get the wrong impression. Nurse Whitely was not a shirker. When she reported ill and unable to come in yesterday evening, no one queried it. She had fainted the day before; she was pregnant.' The only explanation for her presence on the path where she had been attacked, that Sister Bascombe could see, was that she had felt better, changed her mind and decided to go to work after all.

Had her attacker, expecting her to be on that shift, been waiting in the hope that she would be alone, Tansey wondered. Or had he met her by chance? Or was he her lover, and she had come to meet him? And the most vital question – was there any connection with the killing of Father Le Merle? It was difficult to believe there was not some link between the two deaths, but ... Dick Tansey reproached himself. He was wasting time worrying, like a dog at a bone, at questions to which there were at present no answers. He asked the girl from the administration office, whom Bernard Cross had assigned to him as a runner, if she would please fetch Dr Quentin.

'Good morning,' he said when Peter Quentin arrived. 'I'm sorry to interrupt your work. I'm sure you're busy.'

'I'm always busy.' Quentin sat down in the chair Tansey indicated, and stretched his long legs in a vain effort to appear relaxed.

'Perhaps you would tell me how you came to find Nurse Whitely's body,' Tansey said, and, when Quentin had explained, added, 'You must be very observant, Doctor. I gather other people had passed along there without noticing the red of a nurse's cloak that alerted you.'

'There were a couple of nurses in front of me, but they were deep in conversation. I just realized that the red colour was the same as the lining of cloaks the nurses wear.'

Quentin shrugged and deliberately looked at his watch. This annoyed Tansey. He realized that everyone was making a great effort to keep the hospital running smoothly, but he too had work to do, and he resented the young man's arrogance. He thought of Spenser's broad hint.

'Nurse Whitely was a friend of yours,' he said, scarcely making it a question.

'A friend? No, Superintendent. I don't know what gave you that idea. I knew her, of course. I had worked with her, and with many of the other nurses in the hospital.'

'You dated her. Do you date many of the nurses?'

'Quite a few, Superintendent. A meal, the cinema, a drive into the country, nothing spectacular.'

'And sex?'

'If it's willingly given.' Quentin threw up his hands in surrender. 'Okay, Superintendent, I know there's been gossip about me and Kathy Whitely. I was rather taken by her. I dated her once, spent more money on her than was my wont. But she was a cold little bitch, wouldn't even kiss me goodnight, and then spread the story that I tried to rape her. Believe me, I care too much for my career prospects to try a fool thing like that.'

Reluctantly Tansey believed him, but Quentin had given himself a good reason for disliking Nurse Whitely. 'I have to ask you, Dr Quentin,' he said. 'Where were you yesterday evening?'

Quentin gave a wry smile. 'I have no alibi, Superintendent. I was at home in my digs, studying, and my landlady was out.'

'Fair enough,' Tansey said. 'Let's forget Nurse Whitely for the moment. You're a Roman Catholic, I understand. You knew Father Le Merle?'

'The answer to both those questions is yes – and no. My mother was a Catholic and I was brought up a Papist. When I have to state my religion I say RC because it's simpler and avoids argument, but I no longer practise. In fact, I'm an agnostic, if anything. When I came to Colombury, Father Le Merle would have welcomed me as one of his flock, but naturally I refused. He took it fairly well and said that if I ever wanted him I knew where to find him. However, I never felt the need, and of course it's too late now.'

'Right,' Tansey said. 'Thank you for answering my questions so helpfully, Dr Quentin.'

Quentin looked at him. 'Aren't you going to ask me where I was last Saturday when the good priest met his untimely death, Superintendent?'

'No, Dr Quentin. But I expect you'll tell me.'

'Okay! I don't see why the hell I should, but I was in the Windrush Arms about what I gather was the time of the stabbing. I dare say someone will remember me.'

'I dare say, Dr Quentin.' Tansey pushed back his chair to indicate the interview was over. 'After all, we know where to find you if necessary.'

'You do, Superintendent, yes.' Quentin got to his feet. 'I'm not about to disappear like Alfred Yorke, whom none of the great Thames Valley Police Force seem able to find.'

He nodded his farewell and went, leaving Tansey to wonder which of them had won that round.

When Superintendent Tansey asked next for Nurse Gemma Drayton he was told she was not on duty until the evening. Sister Bascombe telephoned the nurses' home on his behalf, but only to learn that Gemma Drayton had been very upset when she learnt of Kathy Whitely's murder, and had gone for a walk. This annoyed Tansey, who wondered if the girl was deliberately avoiding a meeting with him, and further questioning.

In this he was right. Gemma wanted to think. She hadn't lied to the detectives when Tansey and Whitelaw had interviewed her, but she hadn't told them the whole truth – or what she believed to be the whole truth. She had promised Kathy, and she had kept her promise. But now Kathy was dead. She couldn't question Kathy. She would have to make up her own mind.

It seemed to her as she set off across the fields in the direction of Coriston College that Kathy's death must be connected with that of Father Le Merle. There could be no other reason than that the killer feared that Kathy suspected him, or knew something that would betray him. But in that case Kathy had lied to her. Kathy had denied being in

St Stephen's church on Saturday evening at the time the priest had been killed; indeed, she denied ever having been inside the church. She had said that as it was her free day she had taken the opportunity to go into Oxford, in order to make enquiries about having a private abortion if she decided not to marry Brian Minton. Because it was cold she had been wearing her nurse's cloak over ordinary clothes. She had been late getting back to Colombury, had been further delayed by meeting Peter Quentin, and had been running to catch the bus to Little Chipping and have supper with her parents when she bumped into Gough and the *Courier* man, Carson, at the end of the lane beside the church.

Kathy had told Gemma that she refused to go to the police because she knew nothing that would help them, and she was in enough hassle as it was with her unwanted pregnancy. Then, when all the nurses were questioned, creating some havoc in the hospital, she had been afraid to come forward because she knew Mr Cross would blame her for delaying and causing an extra complication.

Suddenly Gemma, who had been walking at a fair pace, stopped dead. She had seen a flaw in her reasoning. Kathy need not have been in the church. The killer might merely have seen her running from that direction and assumed she had been there. But on such slim evidence, would he have been prepared to kill her? If the answer was yes, then he could be prepared to kill Kathy's friend in whom she might have confided. Gemma shivered with fear as she realized that she herself might be in danger.

CHAPTER 10

Nurse Drayton sat opposite Superintendent Tansey and wept. Great tears rolled down her cheeks and she gulped for breath. Sergeant Abbot felt sorry for her; Tansey did not.

'I hope you realize, Miss Drayton, that if you had produced this evidence before, Kathleen Whitely might still be alive? If it had been made public that Miss Whitely had *not* been in St Stephen's church and couldn't help in any way with the police investigation into Father Le Merle's death, there would probably have been no reason to kill her.'

Gemma nodded, and Tansey thought that it was not really the girl's fault. The *Courier* was more to blame; it was the paper that had blown up the story about the nurse and, he admitted to himself, the publicity about the police inquiries at the hospital hadn't helped either.

'But it was primarily Kathy's own fault,' he said more gently. 'She should have told Inspector Whitelaw the truth. However, it's no use repining about all that now. We don't know for sure – there may have been another motive – but it's a fair assumption that the purpose of killing Kathy was to stop her from going to the police. The point is, who could have suspected it was Kathy, and not some other nurse, who might have incriminating evidence? She told you that it was she who collided with Gough and Carson in the lane, though she hadn't been in the church, but you say you didn't repeat the story to anyone.'

Tansey paused to let this sink in, and then continued, 'Now, who else might Kathy herself have told? Please think, my dear. This is important. The killer of Father Le Merle *knew* that Kathy was the nurse we were looking for, and it doesn't matter that she couldn't incriminate him, if he

91

thought that she might. Apart from you, who else might have known?'

Gemma wiped her eyes and tried to compose herself. 'I see the point and I'm sorry I wasn't quite frank earlier. To answer your question, well, Dr Quentin for one. I'm not sure where she ran into him that evening, but he could have seen in which direction she was heading. Then there's her boyfriend, Brian Minton, who works in Barclays Bank. And I suppose Steve Poole is a possibility. She used to go around with him before Brian appeared on the scene, and they're still friends. I can't think of anyone else, but I suppose it could have been mentioned casually – and passed on.'

'It's a possibility. And thank you,' Tansey said. 'That should help for a start. Now, just one more question. You say Kathy assured you that she had not been in St Stephen's. Did it cross your mind that she might not have been telling you the truth?'

Gemma took her time about answering this. 'Not at first, no. But when I told her she ought to admit it was her who bumped into those two chaps at the corner of the lane, it annoyed her. She said it was all right for me, as I'd been on duty. It wouldn't be me who would have to face the fuss and blow with the police. So it occurred to me later that perhaps she had been in the church but was afraid that, if she told me, I might give her away, in spite of my promise.' Gemma shook her head. 'I'm not sure.'

'That's fine, Miss Drayton. Thank you once again,' Tansey said, and indicated that the interview was over.

At the door Gemma hesitated. 'I can't help worrying. I'm scared – for myself.'

'I don't really think you need to be afraid.' Tansey was not unsympathetic. 'I would advise you, as I would anyone connected with this case, however remotely, not to go out alone after dark. But I intend to inform all the media at once that either Kathy's death was completely separate from Father Le Merle's, or that Kathy was mistakenly murdered as she had not been in the church and there was no reason to suppose that she or any nurse knew anything about Father

Le Merle's death. That, I hope, will take the heat off all the nursing staff.'

'Yes, I'm sure it will. Thank you,' Gemma said, and fled.

Superintendent Tansey was as good as his word. The police belief that the killing of Father Le Merle and the killing of Nurse Kathleen Whitely were either two completely disconnected events or the result of a misunderstanding on the part of the killer, was made clear on television and radio news and in the press. The *Courier* next day made a big thing of it, taking a share of the credit for what it called 'a piece of brilliant deduction from information received'.

It was a pity that Tansey could not have known how the news item – and, important though it was, it was little more than that – was variously received. He would have been interested in the differing reactions, among them those of Brian Minton and his mother.

'You realize what will happen now, don't you, Brian?' Mrs Minton said after they had listened to the local radio news over breakfast. 'The police will be around here asking you questions. As long as they thought that girl was killed because she knew something about the priest's death, you were in the clear, but not any more. The motive's got something to do with her private life – and her private life includes you.'

'The news reader didn't completely rule out the connection between the deaths, Ma,' Brian protested. 'He said –'

'I heard what he said!' Mrs Minton was a big and forceful woman, covering her present fears by a show of bluster. 'You ought never to have got involved with that little tart. Aren't there plenty of nice girls at the bank?'

'Yes, Ma, but I – I loved Kathy.'

'Love!' Mrs Minton snorted. 'You listen to me, Brian. Kathy was just a girl you knew. There was nothing serious between you. On Thursday you came straight home from the bank and you didn't go out all the evening. I can vouch for that.'

'But you can't. You –'

'Understand, Brian?' Mrs Minton stamped her foot.

'Yes, Ma. I understand,' Brian Minton said miserably.

93

He went up to his room and wondered what to do. He knew what he ought to do, indeed what he should have done already. He should have gone to the police, and it wasn't too late for that even now. But he would have to face his mother's anger, and Kathy was no longer there to give him support. His mother would always win.

So, when Superintendent Tansey and Sergeant Abbot called on the Mintons later that Saturday morning, Brian accepted the alibi his mother gave him for Thursday evening. He made light of his relationship with Kathy Whitely, and denied that she had told him anything about her movements on the previous Saturday; he hadn't seen her for days before then.

'You know what it's like in a small town, Superintendent,' Mrs Minton said. 'The gossip! A boy has only to take a girl out once and they're engaged.'

'But you were not engaged, not even unofficially, to Miss Whitely?' Tansey looked at Brian speculatively.

'No, I was not.'

'And the baby she was carrying was not yours?'

This time Brian didn't have to deny it. His mother spoke for him. 'Certainly not! How dare you suggest such a thing, Superintendent? The girl was a – a tart. You'd better ask that Steve Poole, or one of the doctors from the hospital.'

'We shall continue our inquiries in all directions, I assure you, Mrs Minton,' Tansey said, and after five more minutes was happy to make his escape.

'What a woman!' he said to Abbot as they drove away from the Mintons' house. 'What a harridan! Poor Brian. You can't blame him. He lied through his teeth, but so did she. Why, I ask myself, why?'

Abbot could think of no sensible answer to this, and took the question as rhetorical. 'Who next, sir?' he asked. 'The physio, Steve Poole? He lives in a flat over the cleaners in the High Street with his girlfriend, Tracey Moore.'

'Fine, Sergeant. We can leave the car at the police station. What does Miss Moore do?'

'She's a school teacher, sir.'

Tansey noticed Abbot stifle a grin, but didn't comment. He understood it when the door to the flat was opened by the 'school teacher'. She was slightly under six feet, with long corn-coloured hair and wide violet eyes, and she was dressed in a bright green towel that just managed to cover her from her breasts to the top of her thighs.

'Superintendent Tansey and Sergeant Abbot,' Tansey said.

'Steve!' the girl called. 'Steve, the fuzz are here. Come in, guys,' she added, her voice low and husky.

She showed them into a large room, furnished in vivid colours and shapes, where Poole greeted them in a striped cotton bathrobe. 'Good morning,' he said. 'We were expecting you, Superintendent, but not quite so early. And yes, Kathy Whitely was my girlfriend at one time. We broke up by mutual consent, but we continued to have the odd drink together. And no, I did not make her pregnant. Nor did I kill her. When I last saw her, which was on Wednesday, she was lying on the floor in a corridor at the hospital with Mr Ritchie and Gemma Drayton bending over her. She'd fainted, and knocked a whole trolley of equipment over, but she was very much alive.'

'Thank you for that information,' Tansey said, 'but I'm afraid I'll need more detail.'

Before Poole could speak, the girl said, 'I'm going to get our brunch, Steve. If you want me, give a shout. That goes for you, too, Superintendent, though I can't imagine how I can help you.'

'A tactful young lady,' Tansey said as she departed. 'Now, Mr Poole, tell me more about your relationship with Kathy Whitely.'

Steve Poole shrugged. 'I met her at the hospital in the course of work, and asked her for a date. We went together for a year, but her shifts made planning anything difficult, and frankly I found this irritating. Then last spring the art teacher at Coriston College had a heart attack, and Tracey came to replace him.'

'And to replace Kathy?'

'Sure, but Kathy was already dating that wimp, Minton,

95

so there were no hard feelings. Ask anyone. Ask Gemma Drayton. Kathy and I stayed friends.'

'All right, Mr Poole,' Tansey said. 'Just one or two more questions. Did you know Father Le Merle?'

'By sight. He was often around the hospital. But not otherwise.' Steve Poole relaxed, glad of the change of direction that Tansey's probing seemed to be taking. 'Le Merle wasn't really interested in physio patients. The very sick, and those frightened by what might be wrong with them, or those about to have an operation – they were more his line. But, Superintendent, I don't understand. According to the media, which is all I've gathered about the case, Kathy was killed for some personal reason or because the killer believed, rightly or wrongly, that she could incriminate him in Father Le Merle's death – which, it was made clear, she could not.'

'Which theory would you accept?' Tansey asked.

Steve Poole gave the point some thought. 'The second,' he said at last. 'I can't conceive of any reason for killing poor Kathy otherwise.'

Privately Tansey agreed, but there was no evidence to support him. He nodded. 'Right, Mr Poole. A final question then. Where were you on Thursday evening?'

'Here, in this flat. I had paperwork to do which detained me, so I left the hospital later than usual – after six – and came straight home. I had a couple of drinks, cooked myself supper, watched television, then wrote a few letters and went to bed quite early.'

'You were alone. Miss Moore was not with you?'

'Unfortunately not at what I gather is the relevant time. She came in much later – not until after eleven. There was some bash for parents at Coriston on Thursday, and all the staff had to be there, including Tracey.'

'No one dropped in on you? No one phoned?'

'No, Superintendent, I have no kind of alibi. But I repeat that I did not kill Kathy, and I hope you catch whoever did.'

Tansey dropped Abbot off at his parents' house and, after a brief visit to the incident van to make sure that vigilance for any sign of Alfred Yorke in the neighbourhood had not abated, had a solitary lunch at the Windrush Arms. He planned to pay what amounted to a courtesy visit to Mr and Mrs Whitely in Little Chipping, and then to call it a day. He was determined to get home early; his son was having a birthday party and he had promised to be there.

The Whitelys lived in one of the cottages on the straggling main street of Little Chipping, next door to the pub where, according to Abbot, Colin Whitely spent a lot of his time. However, today, in response to a phone call telling them of the superintendent's intended visit he was at home, watching football on television. Mrs Whitely turned off the set immediately.

'Colin, can't you see the superintendent is here?' she demanded.

'Good afternoon, sir,' Colin Whitely said; he was a frail-looking wreck of a man. 'Excuse me not getting up, but it's difficult for me.' He gestured towards a stick that was propped against his chair.

'It's the result of the accident he had in the army,' Gwen Whitely explained.

'They blew me up,' Colin Whitely said bitterly. 'It was meant to be manoeuvres, with a grenade practice, not real war, but some bugger got it wrong. Nothing's ever gone right for us since, and now we've lost our Kathy.'

'Yes, that was tragic,' Tansey said. 'I offer you my sincere condolences. I have children of my own and I'd hate to lose either of them. But at least it may be a little consolation to you to know that Kathy's death was quick and she didn't suffer.'

'She was a good girl,' Gwen Whitely said; her eyes, red and inflamed, bore witness to how much she had wept for her daughter, and undoubtedly there would be more tears to come. 'We were proud of her, a nurse, responsible for looking after a whole ward at night quite often.'

'I could kill the bugger that did it, with my bare hands,' Whitely said, though to Tansey he didn't look capable of killing a mouse. He paused, and then enquired bluntly, 'Did he rape her?'

'No,' Tansey assured him, and was thankful to be asked

no further questions; there was no other reply he could give, though he was well aware that the truth, whatever it was, would be made clear at the inquest.

'I always hoped she'd marry a doctor,' Gwen Whitely said sadly, thinking of her dreams for Kathy. 'She had a lot of admirers, you know, Superintendent. She was a very pretty girl, though I must admit I didn't think she was looking her best when she came to supper last Saturday. It's dreadful that we'll never see her again.'

'Yes,' Tansey said. He had done his duty by the Whitelys, and all he wanted now was to get away from the pathetic couple. There was nothing he could do for them, except catch their daughter's killer. 'It was fortunate that she worked in Colombury. You must have been able to see quite a lot of her,' he continued, voicing platitudes and preparing to take his leave.

'That was thanks to the brigadier,' Whitely said, 'like so much else. He arranged for Kathy to come to the hospital nearest to us. He's a governor.'

'Brigadier – Wessex?' Tansey enquired.

'I had served under him earlier in the army,' Whitely said. 'He was very good to me when the accident happened. He saw I got the best possible attention, though my condition was no fault of his, and he helped me to get a better pension than I would have done, by swearing to the great extent of my disabilities.'

'He's a very kind man,' said Gwen Whitely.

'But –' Tansey started. He was sure Whitely was mistakenly grateful to Wessex, but he told himself that it was no business of his. Nevertheless, he said, 'Brigadier Wessex stood up for you at the Medical Board, did he?'

'He was on the Board, sir. He knew what he was talking about and he swayed them in my favour.'

'Brigadier Wessex was an officer in the Royal Army Medical Corps?' Tansey realized that this was the only explanation.

'Yes, of course, sir.'

The Whitelys stared at the superintendent. Here was a fact that everyone knew, but apparently he did not. They couldn't understand it. Tansey didn't blame them. He blamed himself. He had had few dealings with the military and it had simply not occurred to him to enquire in what regiment Brigadier Wessex had served. He wondered who else among the conceivable suspects – apart from the obvious people at the hospital – had the medical knowledge that Ghent suspected the murderer of Father Le Merle possessed. He determined to find out, however belatedly, but there were other things on his mind. He said goodbye to the Whitelys, once more offered his condolences, and set off to collect Sergeant Abbot. He was going to be in good time for Peter's birthday party.

The party ended at last. An over-excited small boy and his younger sister were finally asleep. Their parents, having cleared up the débris and having had a couple of drinks and supper, were also in bed by now. Hilary, who had borne the brunt of the party, had at once fallen asleep, but Tansey was restless. Against his will, he found himself reviewing the deaths of Father Le Merle and Kathy Whitely, convinced in his own mind that they were connected, though he had no real reason to think so.

Father Le Merle had been killed on the Saturday evening. On Monday, the *Courier* had run the story of the nurse, and all the nurses at the hospital had been interviewed. Between the weekend and the following Thursday, Kathy had been identified as the nurse in question and someone had decided that she was a genuine threat and must be eliminated. But when and how had she been identified? The only way to find the answer, which might well tell him who had killed her, Tansey thought as he drifted off to sleep, was to retrace Kathy's life during that week, a task that would keep Maurice Whitelaw busy for a day or two.

CHAPTER 11

'There is a Mr Timothy Cantley at the enquiry desk, asking to see you, sir.' The officer sounded amused. 'He insists it should be you and no one else.'

'Did he say what his business was?'

'It's in connection with the deaths of Father Le Merle and the nurse, sir, so I gather.'

Superintendent Tansey frowned. It was Monday morning, one of those grey days which make for a bad start to an ominous week. He was busy going through his paperwork and giving his secretary instructions. Soon he would have to drive into Oxford to attend the postmortem of Kathleen Whitely. He could do without an unwelcome visitor, certainly one of whom he had never heard. Nevertheless, he couldn't risk missing what might be a lead.

'All right,' he said resignedly. 'I'll send someone down to collect him.' He glanced at his secretary. 'Would you mind?'

'Of course not, sir.'

And a few minutes later, after a brief knock on the door, she announced Mr Timothy Cantley and withdrew. Tansey was left staring in surprise at a small boy in grey flannel trousers and a Coriston College blazer.

'Good morning, sir,' said the boy, who appeared to be completely self-possessed.

'Good morning, Mr – er Cantley,' Tansey said, keeping his face straight with difficulty. 'Please sit down and tell me why you wanted to see me.'

'Thank you, sir,' he said. 'You see, my father always taught me that if I wished to achieve anything I should go to the top. So I thought I should come to you.'

Tansey regarded Timothy Cantley quizzically. He wasn't sure what to make of him. The boy, he guessed, was about twelve. He had a round childish face and wore large spectacles which gave him a typically owlish expression, but he looked and sounded intelligent, and there was no doubt about his composure.

'Your father gave you wise advice,' Tansey said.

'He is wise – most of the time,' Timothy replied.

'So I'm sure he also told you that you should never waste people's time, Mr Cantley.' Tansey was becoming a trifle impatient.

Timothy grinned, revealing a wide gap between his two front teeth, which made him look even more child-like. 'Yes, sir. Well, I wanted to put you straight, sir, because you haven't got it right about that nurse, Kathy Whitely. She did go into St Stephen's church the evening Father Le Merle was killed. I saw her.'

'You're quite sure?' Tansey spoke sharply. 'You know Nurse Whitely, do you?'

'Yes. I had a bad accident on my bike last year. Not really serious, but I spent a couple of weeks in the hospital and I got to know Nurse Whitely and Dr Quentin, because they were the people who were mainly looking after me. They didn't seem to get on too well together then, and they were quarrelling, or at least arguing, again that Saturday evening.'

Superintendent Tansey regarded Mr Timothy Cantley shrewdly. The boy might just have blown the case wide open. Alternatively, he could have invented the whole story – or most of it – though there was the fact Gemma Drayton had mentioned that by chance Kathy had met Quentin that evening.

'Timothy,' he said, dropping the absurd practice of calling the boy 'Mr Cantley'. 'The police receive a lot of information from various sources, some of it –'

'From snouts, you mean? I'm not a snout, sir, obviously, but I wouldn't mind a reward if there's one going. I had to spend my own money to get here by bus, and there'll be trouble at Coriston. I'm a weekly boarder, and I should be back there right now.'

Tansey laughed. 'We'll see. I agree you shouldn't be out of pocket, but I need more information. Where did you see Dr Quentin and Kathy Whitely on Saturday evening? What time? Were you alone? What were you doing? Why do you say they were arguing? Can anyone else confirm your evidence?'

With very little prompting, Timothy Cantley produced a clear and logical account. He had been skulking – his word – near the cinema between five and half-past; he wasn't sure of the time. There was a film he wanted to see, but under-sixteens had to be accompanied by an adult, and he had been hoping to find an accommodating couple ready to adopt him for the evening when Dr Quentin and Nurse Whitely had come along. He had been about to speak to them when he saw they were arguing – he could tell by the way they gestured, he said – so he had drawn back into the doorway of the butcher's shop next to the cinema until they had gone by.

'As they passed me, I heard Nurse Whitely say, "Go away, Peter. Can't you take no for an answer?" and he said, "You'll regret it, Kathy."'

'Timothy!' Tansey protested. 'This could be important. You really heard that? You haven't made it up? Dr Quentin said, "You'll regret it, Kathy"?'

'That's right, sir. I promise you. I heard them clearly,' the boy insisted. 'I know it sounds bad for Dr Quentin, but it wasn't like that. He didn't sound angry. It was more as if he was teasing her.'

'I see.' Tansey was doubtful. He didn't know what to believe. Timothy Cantley didn't strike him as a liar, but the boy might easily have let his imagination run away with him, and anyhow, was he capable of interpreting what he had heard? 'Okay, Timothy, what happened next?'

'I'd given up on the film. I decided to go home. Nurse Whitely had run off, and I followed her because I was going that way. I saw her go into St Stephen's. I've no idea where Dr Quentin went.'

Timothy spoke earnestly, his brow wrinkled as he tried to recall the scene. 'There weren't many people about, but I remember passing that chap called Jason something, who's not too bright. Do you know who I mean, sir?'

'Yes,' Tansey said. 'His name is Jason Clark.' He hesitated. 'I suppose you didn't see a man in a raincoat coming out of the church, did you, Timothy?'

'No, sir, not that I remember.' Timothy shook his head firmly. 'Jason wasn't wearing a raincoat.'

'Right,' Tansey said. 'Now, if you've nothing else to tell me, I've just one more question. Why have you been so long in coming to me?'

'I've been at school all the week. It's a different world there, sir. I didn't know you wanted information about Nurse Whitely until I came home on Friday night and – and she was dead by then. She was so – so nice.' For the first time Timothy Cantley showed emotion, but he was not going to cry. He swallowed hard. 'Then there was that report in the Saturday *Courier* which I knew was wrong, but I couldn't get away until today, and, as I say, there'll probably be a row because I'm here now when I should be back at college.'

'I expect I can fix that,' Tansey said, producing a ten-pound note from his wallet. 'After all, you've been a great help to the police, as any good citizen should be. This will recompense you for your trouble, and we'll send you back to school in a police car. You may have to make a formal statement later, but, if so, we'll let you know. All right?'

'Brilliant!' Timothy said, his eyes shining. 'Thank you very much, sir.'

'Thank you, Mr Cantley,' Tansey said gravely.

A little later, watching Dr Ghent carve up Kathy's body with expertise and a total disregard for her humanity, while he muttered to his assistant, Superintendent Tansey brooded on what he had learnt from Timothy Cantley. Before leaving headquarters Tansey had passed the boy's story on to Inspector Whitelaw, who had been inclined to be sceptical about its veracity. But on the whole Tansey had decided to trust it. There was already part corroboration from Gemma Drayton, and Dr Quentin, when questioned again, should be able to confirm more – if he were willing to co-operate.

'Finished!' Ghent announced, rousing Tansey from his thoughts. 'And how interesting it was! I'll just wash up and then I'll tell you about it over coffee.'

'Fine,' Tansey said. He knew Ghent well enough not to press him with questions, which would have been counter-productive, and he curbed his own impatience until the pathologist was prepared to reveal his findings, or as many of them as he thought need not wait for his report.

'Interesting,' Ghent repeated, having first tasted his coffee. 'I'll spare you the female, well-nourished, approximately three months pregnant stuff, Superintendent, and get to the cause of death, which is much more important. She was strangled. The killer wore gloves. No noticeable fingerprints.'

'Oh!' said Tansey, who had been expecting a piece of information that Ghent would have considered fascinating, even if it proved useless from the point of view of the investigation.

Dr Ghent smiled. 'My dear Superintendent, don't be disappointed. There's more to come. As you're aware, the victim was clearly attacked on the path and dragged into the bushes. Nothing unusual about that. The signs were self-evident. Any amateur detective could have deduced it.'

'I had got so far,' Tansey said drily.

'Sure,' Ghent agreed. 'What you didn't know, couldn't know, was that almost certainly the attacker originally had no intention of dragging her into the bushes. He didn't want to rape her, assault her in any way – there's no sign of anything like that. He just wanted to kill her neatly, cleanly, as I have no doubt he killed Father Le Merle.'

Tansey drew a deep breath. He didn't much like Dr Ghent, with his expensive cars and exotic holidays, and his disregard of other people's convenience. But he had implicit faith in the doctor's ability as a pathologist. Ghent didn't make his pronouncements lightly.

'The girl has a horrific bruise on the back of her neck, for which there would seem to be only one explanation,' Ghent said. 'The killer came from behind and chopped her with the edge of his hand at just the right place, with the intention of

104

hitting the spinal cord and thus causing almost instantaneous death.'

'But you said she had been strangled,' Tansey objected.

'So she was. Either some instinct made her turn as he struck or the collar of her nurse's cloak gave her some protection, but it was not a death blow,' Ghent said. 'I would guess that she was knocked to the ground and was pretty well senseless when he dragged her off the path and completed his work. After all, there were no signs of a struggle, but it was not a nice clean killing like Father Le Merle's.'

'You keep on comparing the two deaths, Dr Ghent. Why? They're quite different methods,' Tansey said.

'Isn't it obvious?' Ghent was at his most superior. 'They both show a knowledge of human anatomy. The knife thrust that did for the priest might have been chance, but when the second killing shows a similar expertise, chance can surely be ruled out. It follows that both the murders were performed by someone with more than a modicum of professional training, at least in my opinion.'

Superintendent Tansey was not about to question Ghent's opinion, not in this field. 'The killer seems to have been too clever for his own good,' he said. 'He's pointed the finger at himself, in a sense. Unfortunately, most of the suspects have some kind of medical know-how.'

'I would say your man has more than that, Superintendent. Doesn't something else strike you about these two killings?'

Tansey hesitated. 'They're both cold-blooded, bold, efficient,' he ventured.

'Yes, efficient is the word, even though the second one didn't go exactly according to plan,' Ghent agreed. 'He didn't just have a cursory knowledge of the pressure points, such as he might have acquired from a medical journal. He planned to have as little contact as possible with his victim, knowing the dangers that DNA inquiries can present, but he made sure that both Le Merle and Whitely were dead before he left them. It all adds up to the fact that he is a very dangerous man because he knows precisely what he's doing. Let's hope he doesn't intend to kill anyone else.'

*　　　*　　　*

105

While Superintendent Tansey was listening to Dr Ghent's analysis of the murderer, Inspector Whitelaw had driven to Colombury. His instructions had been vague; he was to try to trace Kathy Whitely's movements from the Saturday of Father Le Merle's death to the Friday morning when her body was found.

It was a tedious and probably unprofitable task covering a lot of old ground, and privately Whitelaw thought that it could have been assigned to Sergeant Donaldson. Tansey thought otherwise. He wanted not only Maurice Whitelaw's thoroughness, but also his intuitive ability to spot anomalies and seize on any seemingly uncharacteristic behaviour. If the inspector sometimes lacked imagination as to where his findings might lead, that didn't matter; Tansey could provide imagination himself.

Whitelaw parked his car behind the police station and first retraced what, according to Timothy Cantley, had been Kathy's steps on her return from Oxford on Saturday evening. Physically the surroundings fitted the boy's description; his account could have been accurate. Reaching St Stephen's, Whitelaw went inside and sat in a pew at the rear of the church near the door. It was approximately where Kathy would have sat if she had slipped out when Brigadier Wessex turned on the lights and where, if the killer had come straight down the side aisle from the sacristy, he would have almost brushed past her as he left. But, except for the candles at the far end of the building, it would have been dark then.

'Good morning, Inspector.'

Whitelaw turned, startled; he hadn't heard anyone come into the church, but Father Hanson was standing beside him. 'Good morning,' he said. 'You surprised me.'

'I'm sorry. I came to make sure there was no one in the church. We've just had a letter from the bishop with instructions that unless there's a service it's to be kept locked. I think he was upset by Brigadier Wessex's letter, and after all the publicity about Father Le Merle's murder –'

'What letter, Father?'

Hanson sat down beside the inspector. 'It seems that the

Brigadier lodged a complaint against Father Le Merle because of the way he allowed Alfred Yorke to use St Stephen's as a dosshouse,' he said hesitantly. 'There was bitter feeling about it, you know, Inspector, among members of the congregation and so as a member of the council the Brigadier was fully within his rights. Actually we've not seen Yorke here since Father Le Merle was ... was killed, but he might turn up again and as he's wanted by the police it would mean more publicity that we could do without.'

'Yes, I understand your bishop's point of view,' said Whitelaw, affably. 'Involvement with murder, however innocent one may be, is never to be desired. Which reminds me, Father Hanson, where did you spend the early part of Thursday evening?'

Hanson was taken aback at the twist the conversation had taken, 'I – er – Thursday, when Nurse Whitely was killed? That was the day Father Le Merle's brother came to see me. He went back to Oxford after tea and Father Sinclair was taking a confirmation class in the church, so I was alone.'

'What about your housekeeper?'

'Mrs Faudin?' Hanson shrugged. 'I could have gone out without her knowing – but I didn't, Inspector. I did not kill the poor girl! I didn't kill anyone!'

'All right, Father Hanson. Just a couple more questions. First, have you ever studied medicine, considered becoming a doctor, perhaps?'

Hanson stared at the inspector. 'The answer is no. My eldest brother is a doctor and he used to tell us all sorts of gory details when he was training, which were enough to put off anyone from a medical career.'

Whitelaw laughed. 'But he taught you some knowledge of how the body works?'

'I can tell the difference between a tibia and a fibia, if that's what you mean, but –'

'I was only joking, Father,' Whitelaw lied. 'The other question is did you know Nurse Whitely?'

'Yes, Inspector,' Hanson said unexpectedly. 'I knew her quite well. She was one of my nurses when I was rushed to hospital with peritonitis six or seven months ago. Gemma

Drayton was another. They used to giggle together. They thought it funny that they should do personal things for a priest, as if a priest doesn't urinate like any other man.'

'Right,' Whitelaw said, and thought that the last ten days had made a difference to Father Hanson; he was much more assured and self-confident now that his difficulties with Belle Sutton had been resolved. 'I'll say goodbye then, and leave you to lock up the church. Thanks for answering my questions.'

Where now? Whitelaw asked himself. He decided on the hospital in the hope of asking Dr Quentin some pointed questions, but there had been a serious car accident and Quentin was busy in casualty. Whitelaw checked Kathy's shifts for the week with Mr Cross and then double-checked them with Sister Bascombe.

As Whitelaw had expected, his morning had been dull and seemingly unproductive. He decided he had had enough and set off for the Pomme d'Or, where he was sure of a welcome and an excellent lunch with his wife's family.

CHAPTER 12

Inspector Whitelaw enjoyed his lunch as much as he had expected, and he was glad of the opportunity to have a word with Mr Gronski over coffee. Before today they hadn't met since Father Le Merle's death, which had greatly upset the Gronskis, who were Catholics and had known the priest personally. Whitelaw had already expressed his sympathy, and now, knowing how much casual information the owners of a restaurant can pick up in the course of their work, he had a question to ask.

'Tell me, Janos,' he said, 'among your patrons, what's the general opinion about these killings?'

Janos Gronski shrugged. 'What you would expect, Maurice. The police are blamed for being slow, especially for not preventing the nurse's murder. As you must know, the public always want miracles. And they think it absurd that the old vagrant, Alfred Yorke, has not been caught.'

'So does our Chief Constable,' said Whitelaw with some bitterness, 'but the wretched man has so far proved too elusive for us, though the whole country's looking for him. I suppose most people think him guilty because he's disappeared, but, between you and me, Janos, the police are keeping an open mind.'

'Quite right too,' Gronski agreed. 'But everyone doesn't blame him. There was a small dinner party here on Saturday night, given by Mr and Mrs Ritchie for the Crosses and two other couples – and they nearly came to blows.'

'What?'

Gronski laughed. 'Maybe I exaggerate a little. However, it was a heated argument. Mr Ritchie started it by saying the police were making it out to be a complex case because they couldn't find Yorke when he was the obvious culprit. This annoyed Mrs Cross, who said that Mr Ritchie was a newcomer to Colombury, he didn't know Alfred Yorke and had no right to judge him. She got very worked up about it, the poor lady, and I really thought for one awful moment that she was going to throw her wine in Mr Ritchie's face. Not what you would wish to happen in a high-class restaurant like the Pomme d'Or. Fortunately, Mr Cross intervened and the crisis passed over. After all, they are meant to be civilized people.'

'Everyone, without exception, has primitive instincts,' remarked Whitelaw.

Fleetingly he wondered why Mrs Cross should have felt so strongly about Alfred Yorke, and thought it was probably due to too much wine. Then, noticing the time, he said a hurried goodbye and thanks to Janos Gronski, and went on his way. He planned to collect his car and pay a call on Brigadier Wessex.

In the event, Inspector Whitelaw's visit to Brigadier Wessex was postponed. He had almost reached the police station when, passing Barclays Bank, he remembered that he was in need of cash and that it was here that Brian Minton, whom Tansey had described as an arrant liar, plied his trade. He went in.

The busy flurry of customers during the lunch hour had become a trickle. There were two cashiers free; one was Brian Minton, his name above his window. Whitelaw approached him and offered him both his Connect Card and, since he was not known at this branch, his warrant card as additional identification.

Minton looked from the warrant card to Whitelaw's face and back again. He wetted his lips. 'Inspector – sir,' he said, his voice low and hoarse. 'I need to talk to you. I must.'

Whitelaw hid his surprise. 'All right, Mr Minton. Fine. When would you like to see me?'

'Now. I could slip out for half an hour.'

'Okay, Mr Minton, if you'll give me my money, I'll wait in my car for you. It's parked behind the police station.'

110

'I – I'll be as quick as I can. Thank you, Inspector.'

Thinking that Kathy Whitely had made a mistake to give up Steve Poole for Brian Minton – if indeed she had – Whitelaw retreated to his car and waited. He was half expecting Minton to change his mind and not turn up, but the young man appeared quite soon as he had promised. However, once seated beside the inspector, he suddenly became tongue-tied.

'Mr Minton,' Whitelaw said at length. 'I'm a busy man and I dare say you can't play truant from your bank for too long, so let's not waste time. Why do you need to talk to me?'

'It's about Kathy. I – I lied to the superintendent. It wasn't like I said it was between Kathy and me. I loved her very much and I wanted to marry her, but my mother –'

'Your mother didn't approve?'

'No. She said I was too young to get married – I'm twenty-four – and that if I really wanted to I could do better than a nurse; that Kathy was – to use Mother's word – flighty, and that such a match would ruin my future prospects.'

'How did you feel about that?' Whitelaw asked, sorry for the wretched Minton.

'As I told you, Inspector, I wanted to marry Kathy, but – you don't know my mother. She's a very strong-minded woman. And then there was the baby.'

'It was your child?'

Minton nodded. 'Yes, I'm sure it was, though I swore to Ma that it wasn't. Inspector, I can't expect you to understand. I've always lived with my mother. I never went away to school or university. My father died when I was a child, and Ma's had to work hard all her life and make sacrifices to get me where I am. But – but she didn't like Kathy, and the whole thing was a quandary for me.'

'Which was solved by Kathy's murder,' Whitelaw commented brutally.

'I didn't want a solution like that! God knows I didn't!' Minton protested.

'Nevertheless, it was convenient,' Whitelaw said, and when Minton made no response, he added, 'Mr Minton, you've admitted that you lied to Superintendent Tansey. Do those lies include your alibi for Thursday evening?'

'Yes, I'm afraid so. I was not at home all the evening with my mother, as I said. Actually *I* was at home, but Ma wasn't,' Minton admitted. 'She was playing bridge with friends. She left me a casserole which I just had to reheat. I had supper, watched television and went to bed. And that's the truth, Inspector, I swear it.'

'Okay, I understand. Now calm down, Mr Minton,' Whitelaw said, not unkindly.

Brian Minton was sweating and wriggling in his seat as if he badly needed to go to the lavatory. He shook his head dispiritedly. 'There's more,' he said. 'I told Superintendent Tansey that I hadn't seen Kathy since Father Le Merle's death, but I really saw her the next day, Sunday. We went for a walk – Ma believed I was with one of my men friends – and Kathy told me she had gone into St Stephen's because she wanted to avoid Dr Quentin, whom she doesn't – didn't – like. She thought she was alone there until someone gave a huge sneeze. Then a minute or two later someone came down the aisle towards her. She was afraid he was going to ask what she was doing, so she buried her face in her hands and pretended to pray, but he just passed by and went out of the door.'

'A pity. It meant she didn't see him. At least she might have told you what he looked like,' Whitelaw said.

'You think it was the murderer – that he'd just killed Father Le Merle?' Minton shuddered.

'I think it highly likely.'

'But if he didn't see her face, she didn't see his either,' Minton reasoned. 'So why should he have killed her – Kathy, I mean? At most, all he would have known was that the girl in the church was a nurse, because she was wearing her cloak, but it was Kathy, my Kathy, he killed.'

Minton's voice broke, and for a moment Whitelaw thought he was going to cry. He gave the young man a little time to control himself, then said that he didn't know why the killer had picked on Kathy. It was the truth, one of the puzzles of the case that he was trying to unravel by retracing Kathy's movements during the week before her death. Not that he was making much progress. There seemed no logical explanation. But there had to be one, he supposed.

'She said that he was close enough to touch,' Minton suddenly blurted. 'And she smelt him.'

'What?'

'She smelt him. She said he had a kind of musty smell that she didn't like.'

'Stop!' Whitelaw, who had been tactfully gazing out of the car window, swung round in his seat. 'Mr Minton, are you absolutely positive, would you swear on oath, that Kathy told you the man who went by her in St Stephen's church on the Saturday evening Father Le Merle was killed had a musty smell about him?'

'That's what Kathy said, Inspector.' Minton stared blankly at Whitelaw.

'Do you know Alfred Yorke?' Whitelaw's voice was hard.

'What? That old tramp? I don't know him. I know of him.' Minton was taken aback. 'I know he usually hangs around Colombury, but he's disappeared and the police are looking for him. What's he got to do with Kathy?'

'He was in the church at the same time as Father Le Merle was killed.'

'Oh! I didn't realize that. And you think he – He always looked dirty. I suppose he would smell.' Minton was at a loss. 'What – what do you want me to do, Inspector?'

'We'll need you to sign a statement, Mr Minton, but it can wait,' Whitelaw said. He leant across the young man and opened the car door for him. 'You'd best be getting back to your bank now, before you lose your job. We'll be in touch. Meanwhile, please keep your mouth shut about this little talk we've had. And thanks for your help. The police appreciate co-operation.'

For a while after Brian Minton had gone Whitelaw sat in his seat and stared out of the window at the neat line of cars in front of him, but he didn't see them. He was thinking hard.

If Kathy had told Minton the truth – and he couldn't

imagine why she would have invented the story – it contradicted the evidence that Yorke had given concerning himself,
but it jibed with what the youth Jason Clark had said. Jason
had maintained that he had seen someone in a raincoat leave
St Stephen's and return there ten to fifteen minutes later.
He had been sure it was the same man, though Tansey had
tried to shake him on that assertion.

Assuming that Minton's evidence, albeit hearsay, and
Jason Clark's were equally acceptable, Yorke could have
killed Father Le Merle, left the church, slipped the knife into
the drain, hidden the chalice somewhere close where he
could retrieve it later, and returned to his pew and his supper.
But it was easy to pick holes in this scenario . . .

There had been no suggestion that the man whom Kathy
had smelt had passed her twice, leaving the church and
returning. The timing, too, was suspect. What was more, the
nature of the killings did not fit Alfred Yorke as there was
nothing frenzied about them, and he was not known to have
any medical expertise; a check had revealed that during his
brief stay up at Oxford he had read medieval history. Above
all, where was the motive? Everyone agreed that Father Le
Merle had been more than charitable to the vagrant.

Whitelaw cursed gently. He knew that the Holy Cow was
putting pressure on Tansey. There had been little news other
than the Colombury murders to exercise the media during
the last few days, and they were concentrating on them
fiercely – and on the inadequacy of the police, though no
one could suggest what more could have been done. But
Tansey needed an arrest, and soon; the worst thing that could
happen was that public opinion, backed by the higher-ups
in the police establishment, should force the arrest of the
wrong man.

Whitelaw started his engine and set off to talk to Brigadier
Wessex.

'Yes, of course, I'm prepared to answer your questions,
Inspector,' John Wessex said testily. 'But I've told you or
Superintendent Tansey all I know, more than once.'

'You've been most helpful, sir, I know,' Whitelaw said in

an attempt to placate the older man. 'However, one or two new points have come up. For instance, we've just learnt that you knew Kathy Whitely.'

The brigadier, who had waved Whitelaw to a chair but had remained standing and was now pacing up and down the room, stopped in his stride. He stared down at the inspector, who was duly thankful that he had never had the misfortune to serve under this officer.

'What the hell has that got to do with anything?' Wessex demanded at last. 'What are you implying, Inspector? You'll be asking me next where I was on Thursday evening when Kathy was killed.'

'All right, sir.' Whitelaw tried to sound casual. 'Where were you?'

The brigadier visibly restrained his irritation but answered the direct question. 'I gather that Nurse Whitely was killed between five and eight in the evening.' He went and sat down. 'I must have left the hospital soon after five. Mr Cross will verify that I was having a business conversation with him. I collected my car and drove home. I was here before six. My wife and the lady who comes in to cook for us when we have a dinner party will vouch for that. Our guests started arriving at half past seven and stayed till about midnight. Among them I might mention were Sir Philip and Lady Midvale.'

'Thank you, sir. I'm sure it won't be necessary to trouble the former Chief Constable,' Whitelaw said. He did not point out that Midvale was no use as an alibi for the earlier part of the evening, when the brigadier by his own admission had been in or near the hospital. 'Actually that's not why I came to see you, sir.'

'Why then? And why mention so ominously that I knew Nurse Whitely? Actually it's her father I know. I've only met the girl a few times.'

'Superintendent Tansey was wondering if you would be free tomorrow evening between 5.15 and 6.30.' Whitelaw ignored Wessex's reference to Kathy Whitely.

'Why? Don't say he's going to offer me a drink.' The

Brigadier laughed; he was making a big effort to throw off his ill humour.

'I'm afraid not, sir. At least, I don't think so.' Whitelaw got his own back by refusing to be amused. 'Superintendent Tansey wishes to have the killing of Father Le Merle re-enacted with as many as possible of the people who were actually in the church about that time. He hopes it might strike a chord in someone's memory that may help us. Would you be available, sir?'

'Tomorrow? Yes, that will be all right, though I doubt if the enterprise will do any good.'

'Thank you, sir. We'll confirm first thing in the morning. We've not asked anyone else yet. And will you please wear – or at least bring – your raincoat? You were wearing a raincoat that Saturday evening, sir?'

'Yes, I was. Is that all?'

'One more thing: the letter you wrote to your bishop about the way Father Le Merle allowed Alfred Yorke to make free of the church. You must have felt very strongly –'

'It was a private and personal letter, which I do not regret. Father Le Merle could not be allowed to go on pampering this vagrant, and letting him desecrate the church. But it's no business of the police whatever, and since Father Le Merle is dead the matter has resolved itself, as the bishop pointed out in his reply to me. However, you may care to know, Inspector, that instructions have been given that except during services the church is to remain locked.'

'So I was informed, sir.'

'Whether this interdict will apply once you have managed to catch Yorke, I don't know. May I ask if you are any nearer to tracing him?'

'Not at the moment, no, sir.'

Whitelaw stood up. He thanked the brigadier for his co-operation and, having reminded him of the appointment for the following evening, took his leave. He left behind him a vaguely disturbed John Wessex, who was far from certain just why the inspector had called on him, and who wondered – stupidly, he told himself – if there was any significance in the request to take his raincoat to St Stephen's.

For Inspector Whitelaw, it was all in a day's work as a detective in the Thames Valley Police Serious Crime Squad, and his thoughts as he drove back to headquarters were centred on the possibility that he might get home reasonably early.

CHAPTER 13

It was not until the following afternoon that Superintendent Tansey and Inspector Whitelaw went to Colombury, but their morning had not been wasted. Tansey had given a press conference, which had pleased no one; inquiries, he commented, were at the moment stalled and, though he claimed to have several promising leads, he admitted to having made little genuine progress.

'Has anyone as much as sighted Alfred Yorke recently?' one of the reporters asked. Another demanded to know whether the woods had been thoroughly searched for him. 'He could be lying up there dead,' the journalist suggested. Yet another wanted to know if he had heard the rumour that Kathy Whitely had been seen going into St Stephen's on the Saturday evening that Father Le Merle had been killed. To this, Tansey, silently cursing, could only reply that he didn't trust rumours.

'Perhaps if you did, you might get somewhere,' a voice from the back of the hall called out.

Tansey ignored the remark, but when the conference ended he knew that he had left the media dissatisfied and that they would take their revenge, which would bring more reproaches from the Chief Constable. That morning's briefing of St John Cowan had not gone well. He, too, wanted action.

'Any damned action!' Tansey said bitterly to Whitelaw when they met in a corridor of headquarters.

'Maybe something will come out of this evening's replay,' Whitelaw said hopefully. 'I've arranged for St Stephen's to be available for us and I've been in touch with all the people we need; they're ready to co-operate.'

'Good,' said Tansey, though he himself was not optimistic that the re-enactment would yield anything of use. 'I'm off now to the inquest on Kathy Whitely. A waste of time. It will be the same as Le Merle's – unlawful killing by a person or persons unknown, but at least it means the body can be released so it's a relief for the family. I'll meet you at St Stephen's at five.'

'Right, sir. I'll have completed the inquiries that were left over from yesterday by then – with any luck. And I'll have the cast assembled.' Whitelaw grinned.

'Luck is not something that's running our way at present,' Tansey said.

Nor did he change his opinion when he reached the Coroner's Court and Tim Spenser of the *Courier* slid into the seat next to him. Spenser had been at the press conference earlier, but for once he had been strangely silent, though Tansey had been too busy parrying questions to notice.

'Could I have a word with you, Superintendent?' Spenser asked with surprising timidity.

'You had your chance at the press conference.' Tansey was not in the best of tempers. 'Stop pestering me.'

Spenser ignored the irritable request. 'If I had asked you about the smell in front of all my colleagues, I'd have forfeited the chance of a scoop, Superintendent. You couldn't expect me to do that, could you?'

'What *smell*?' Tansey asked, though he knew the answer.

'The one poor Kathy smelt as the killer passed her in the church that evening,' Spenser said, keeping his voice low.

'Another rumour!'

'No, sir. Straight from the mouth of Brian Minton.'

'And what made you seek that source?'

'Someone saw him having a heart-to-heart in Inspector Whitelaw's car behind the police station, and tipped me off.'

'I won't ask you who it was, Mr Spenser.' Tansey was angry; Donaldson had been warned several times about leaking information to his cronies on the press, but it did no good. 'I don't need to ask. However, if you've talked to Minton you know as much as we do.'

'I wanted to be sure he wasn't having me on, Superinten-dent. You must admit this musty smell does sound a bit odd, and I didn't want to use it until you'd confirmed it, because it does rather point the finger at your prime suspect, doesn't it? After all, our Alfred is noted for his pong.'

Tansey opened his mouth to deny that he had confirmed or denied anything, and shut it again. The coroner had just entered the court, everyone was standing, and this was not the moment to have an argument with the obnoxious Spenser. But the superintendent was seriously worried. More and more it was being assumed by the public and even by some of the police that Alfred Yorke was the murderer. He wished he could stop the *Courier* from printing the tale of the musty smell which would only add weight to this belief.

Inspector Whitelaw had an early lunch in the canteen and set off for Colombury. There had been no sign of Tansey, who was having a sandwich at his desk. Whitelaw went straight to the hospital, to be greeted by a resigned Bernard Cross.

'I suppose this is just another case for you, Inspector,' he said, 'but personally I shall be glad when it's over. The whole hospital has been upset by it, doctors, nursing staff, patients. One of the nurses – Gemma Drayton, whom you know – swears that she saw Alfred Yorke in Oxford yesterday, but he was looking clean-shaven and quite well dressed. I expect she imagined it.'

Whitelaw was not so sure. A librarian at the Oxford public library had reported to the police that a man more or less answering to Alfred Yorke's description had come into the reference room and enquired how he could discover the names of medical students who had been at the university over a certain period of five years. It was not until he had gone, evidently satisfied with what he had found after some lengthy research, for he had thanked her profusely, that she decided to report the matter. She had explained the delay by saying that the man had been so well-spoken, his manners so good and his appearance so comparatively respectable, that she couldn't relate him to the descriptions in the papers.

But by then, Alfred Yorke, if it had been Alfred Yorke – which Whitelaw was quite prepared to believe – had once more disappeared.

'Nevertheless, I'll have to talk to Nurse Drayton,' Whitelaw said. 'She's an intelligent young woman and, if Yorke has changed his appearance, a fresh description might help.' She might also confirm what the librarian had said, he added to himself.

As always, Bernard Cross was ready to co-operate, but Gemma Drayton could add nothing to the librarian's statement, except to comment that she herself was becoming more and more certain that the man whom she had seen had been Alfred Yorke.

The next interviewee on Whitelaw's list was Dr Peter Quentin, who resented any further questions. He hadn't mentioned seeing Kathy on the Saturday because he hadn't thought it relevant. As for threatening her, that was nonsense; if he had said that she would 'regret it' he must have been referring to her refusal to have a date with him. He had not followed her, so he didn't know if she had gone into St Stephen's church; he had had a drink in the Windrush Arms – the Burkes would probably remember him – and gone home, as he had already told Superintendent Tansey.

Dr Quentin was followed by Steve Poole, who was quite happy to be questioned again, though he couldn't see why it was necessary. He had been off duty on that Saturday, which he had spent with his girlfriend Tracey Moore, who would verify the fact. As for the Thursday evening when Kathy had been killed, he had nothing to add to what he had told Superintendent Tansey, except that he remembered meeting Mr Ritchie, the gynaecologist, who had presumably been on his way to the car park. Ritchie might be able to confirm the time as around six.

Lance Ritchie, caught in a corridor, had difficulty in curbing his irritation. 'What is it now, Inspector?' he demanded. 'In ten minutes, I have to change and wash up for a tricky Caesarean. I can't waste time with you, answering senseless questions which you've already asked once. I wish I'd never gone to that wretched nurse's help when she collapsed with that trolley. As I said, to my knowledge I'd not seen the girl before. I didn't even know her name.'

Whitelaw waited until the tirade had finished. He had some sympathy with the doctor. It was an annoying situation for a busy man, who, through no fault of his own, had become a peripheral witness in a case which meant nothing to him. But there was such a thing as a citizen's duty.

'I'm terribly sorry, sir. It's only a small matter,' Whitelaw apologized. 'Think of the Thursday evening that Nurse Whitely was killed. As you were leaving the hospital, you met a Mr Steve Poole on your way to the car park. Can you tell me what time that was?'

Ritchie took a minute to think. Then he said, 'I can't be accurate, Inspector. My 4.30 patient didn't show up, but I had some paperwork to do. I would say I left the hospital between 5.30 and 6 p.m.'

'Mr Poole put his own departure at around six, sir.'

'Then I'm sure that's when it was, Inspector. I accept what Mr Poole has to say, but I can't vouch for it because I don't know him, even by sight. I've only been at the hospital a few weeks, and frankly my own department has kept me fully occupied.'

'I understand, sir. Thank you very much,' said Whitelaw.

Ritchie nodded and took his departure. His evidence had not surprised Whitelaw. Steve Poole had himself said it was unlikely that Ritchie would have recognized him.

Inspector Whitelaw began to gather his papers together. For the moment he had nothing more to do in the hospital. He decided to go to the incident van, where he could have a cup of tea and work on his report until it was time to meet Tansey in St Stephen's. He was about to leave when there was a sudden tap on the door, and a well-dressed woman whom he didn't know was shown in, followed by an orderly who carried a tray which was set with tea for two and included a plate of chocolate biscuits.

'Good afternoon, Inspector,' she said, gesturing to the orderly to put down the tray. 'I'm Angela Cross. We've not met, but of course you know my husband.'

'Good afternoon, Mrs Cross.'

Whitelaw, who had stood up, reseated himself as Mrs Cross pulled up a chair and started to pour tea. She was a tall, elegant woman with a plain but intelligent face and copper-coloured hair, and she was clearly in command of the situation, though she seemed very tense.

'Milk? Sugar?' she asked.

'Neither, thank you.' Whitelaw was beginning to enjoy himself. 'May I ask why you are giving me tea?'

'A bribe, Inspector.' She smiled, and the smile transformed her face. 'I have a confession to make, and I hoped this might help you to – er – take a lenient view.'

'I very much doubt it, Mrs Cross,' Whitelaw said. 'But it does depend on the nature of the confession.'

Angela Cross took a deep breath. 'Alfred Yorke, the vagrant, the down-and-out who people are saying killed Father Le Merle and Nurse Whitely – he's a relation of mine. Not close. A distant cousin, but when we were children our families *were* close, and Freddie and I were . . . were great friends. We go back a long way, you see, and I've helped him in the past with food and clothes and money. It was the least I could do.'

Mrs Cross paused. In spite of the business about the tea, which had been intended to lighten the occasion, she was by now visibly upset. Whitelaw was afraid of what was to come.

'Have you been sheltering him, Mrs Cross?' he asked gently.

'Not recently. I haven't seen him since Father Le Merle was killed and I've no idea where he might be. But – but, Inspector Whitelaw, I'm sure he didn't kill him or the girl. It's not fair what people are saying, people like Lance Ritchie, who's only just come to Colombury and doesn't know Freddie. The other night at the Pomme d'Or Ritchie was holding forth about it being a cut and dried case, and obviously Yorke was the culprit. I could have hit him.'

'So I've heard, Mrs Cross.'

'You have?' She was startled. 'How?'

'Mrs Cross, the police aren't as inefficient as they may

sometimes seem. We know who Alfred Yorke is, where he went to school and university, and how he came to go to prison for some years.'

Angela Cross was staring at Whitelaw. 'What about me – my relationship to him?'

'We were not aware of that.'

'Were you aware that when he went to prison his family disowned him, that everything was left to his brother who later refused to give him a penny, and none of them has ever done a damn thing for him?' Angela Cross was angry. 'And Freddie's not a bad man. Sure, he was wild when he was young and he killed a man – in a drunken frenzy, the judge agreed – but he's paid for it and I can't believe he would have killed Father Le Merle. He was fond of the priest, and he's a devout Catholic.'

'He has a good advocate in you, Mrs Cross,' Whitelaw said mildly, as she stopped speaking. 'But there is one thing I must ask you. Will you give me your word that, if Alfred Yorke turns up at your house or you learn where he is, you will immediately inform the police, preferably Superintendent Tansey or myself?'

Angela Cross sighed. 'Yes, Inspector, I suppose so. I give you my word. After all, I'm a responsible citizen and I have my husband to consider.' She smiled ruefully. 'I've been telling myself that it was for Bernard's sake I haven't admitted being related to poor Freddie, but that's not altogether true. This is a small gossipy place – Rhoda Ritchie is right about that, even if she ignores Colombury's good qualities – and I wouldn't welcome the talk the news would cause among my friends and acquaintances.'

'I doubt if anyone would in the circumstances, Mrs Cross,' Whitelaw said. 'Incidentally, you have told your husband, haven't you?'

Angela Cross looked guilty. 'Yes, a short while ago,' she admitted. 'And he insisted I should tell you or the superintendent.'

'Good for him,' Whitelaw said, and wondered if the Crosses had had much of an argument about it; Bernard Cross could scarcely have been pleased.

And in fact there had been little new in Mrs Cross's information; most of the vagrant's past history was already known to the police, but the link with Angela Cross was interesting. Alfred Yorke might seek her help again, in which case it was to be hoped that she would keep her word and inform them. Whitelaw was not convinced that she would. There was considerable warmth in her voice when she spoke of 'Freddie', and it was clear that she was fond of him.

Later, when Whitelaw voiced his doubts to Tansey, the superintendent didn't think that much could be done about it. With absences due to leave and injury and sickness, plus the usual over-burden of work, they had no officers free to watch the Crosses' house.

'I suppose we could get Donaldson to make his men keep an eye on the place,' Tansey said doubtfully.

'I'd advise against it,' Whitelaw said, 'for the Crosses' sake. The news would be all around Colombury in no time, and the *Courier* would be on their doorstep.'

Tansey laughed. 'That's for sure,' he said. 'Anyway, I doubt if it's worth the manpower. It's not very likely that Yorke will show up in such an obvious place.'

'Isn't this exciting?' Miss Jean Blair said, her old eyes bright with anticipation.

'It's a little frightening, dear,' said Miss Joan Blair, the fatter and usually more complacent of the two.

Brigadier Wessex glared at the elderly sisters. He wished Superintendent Tansey and Inspector Whitelaw would arrive; the sooner the play-acting was over, the better he would be pleased. He couldn't understand how his wife could stand chatting to Patrick Gough as if they were at a cocktail party and not re-enacting a murder. He couldn't understand why she had insisted on coming with him. He thought the police might think it odd, and he was glad when Lorna Porter came into the church with the doctor. He regretted bitterly the letter he had written to the bishop about Father Le Merle. Without it –

'Do you think this – this replay of events will do any good, Brigadier?' Miss Jean Blair asked with eager curiosity.

'I've no idea,' Wessex said coldly. 'But we are here at the request of the police and it's up to us to co-operate with them as fully as possible.'

'And here they are,' said Miss Joan Blair, 'with Father Hanson and Father Sinclair.'

The police had indeed arrived, in force. The party included Superintendent Tansey, Inspector Whitelaw, Sergeant Abbot and two other police officers – one a woman – from headquarters. In addition, there was Sergeant Donaldson from the Colombury station, accompanied by a very young constable. Tansey immediately took charge.

Striding up the centre aisle, he said, 'Good evening, ladies and gentlemen. Thank you for coming. I hope it hasn't been inconvenient for any of you.'

The remark was greeted by a shaking of heads and smiles; no one wanted to suggest an unwillingness to be helpful to the police. Superintendent Tansey looked around. All those who had been asked were there, with the exception of Dr Ghent, the pathologist, who had said bluntly that he had a previous engagement which he had no intention of cancelling, but his presence was not necessary for what Tansey had in mind.

'In a minute, I'll explain what I want you to do,' Tansey continued. 'This is not an attempt to replay in their entirety the movements of everyone on the Saturday evening when Father Le Merle was killed. Instead, I want to try out a series of, shall we say, experiments, relating to certain aspects of these events. Some of what I shall ask you may seem a little strange, but I assure you there are reasons for it. I am very hopeful this evening will be relevant and useful to the investigation, so I hope you will bear with me.'

He nodded at Whitelaw, who said, 'First, we would like to recreate the timing of various events which took place that evening. This could be extremely important. We may have to do this part of the procedure more than once, but I'll explain the theory, and perhaps we could walk it through. I'm sorry if this sounds as if I were rehearsing a play, but when you remember Father Le Merle and Nurse Whitely you'll accept that we are not doing this for amusement.' To Superintendent Tansey, he added quietly, 'I suppose we should synchronize our watches at this point.'

There was a murmur of assent from those present. Everyone was amenable and Whitelaw, who, in his younger days, had taken part in amateur dramatics, set to work with an efficiency that both gratified and surprised Tansey. Within five minutes everyone was organized. The stand-ins, such as Father Sinclair, who had agreed to represent Alfred Yorke, were in place. The people who had actually been present on that night were waiting, ready, and the others not yet needed were seated in side pews. Privately

Whitelaw cursed the setting of the church, but he had to accept it.

'Now,' he said, trying to strike the right note between the drama of the occasion and the relative absurdity of the present scenario, 'we know that Father Le Merle was alive at approximately 4.30 on that Saturday evening. He and Father Hanson had tea together, as Mrs Faudin, their housekeeper, confirms. Some time before 5.30 Father Le Merle entered the church and went to the sacristy, where the killer found him.'

Whitelaw stopped. He singled out the young local constable, whom Donaldson had brought and whose name was Postgate, and told him what he wanted him to do in a low voice. The youth gawped and the inspector, who reckoned that the constable's IQ was probably even lower that that of Jason Clark, was not displeased. He repeated the instructions.

'Jump to it, then,' interrupted Donaldson, determined to assert his authority. 'We can't wait all night for you.'

'No!' Whitelaw exclaimed. 'Do *not* hurry! Try to walk and act normally, as if you were on an errand for your mum. Do you understand?'

'Yes, sir.' The youth cast a doubtful eye at Donaldson.

As soon as the constable had left, Superintendent Tansey turned up the collar of his raincoat and, head bent, shoulders hunched, followed him. Abbot made a note in his book. The constable, as instructed, had walked a short way down the street and was returning past the church. Tansey had just time to go down the steps and turn away from him and hurry into the nearby lane, from where he watched the constable pass. Then he returned to the church.

'It should take the constable ten to fifteen minutes,' he said.

'Where has he gone?' asked Patrick Gough.

'To the Pomme d'Or, to pick up a cake that has been ordered,' Tansey replied, and nodded to the WPC to wait outside to give him warning of the young man's return.

Someone tittered and Gough flushed to the roots of his

hair. 'I – I'm sorry, sir,' he stammered. 'I didn't mean to intrude.'

'It was a perfectly sensible question,' Tansey said, 'and I answered it as such. He's gone to pick up a cake, which was what a certain witness did on the evening of the murder.'

There was a sudden stillness in the church. It was not as if people had been openly chatting since the police arrived, but there had been the odd whisper, the murmurs of assent or query, the rustle of bodies shifting in not too comfortable pews. Tansey pretended not to notice.

'Now, while we're waiting we'll try something else,' he said cheerfully, and signalled to Whitelaw to continue.

'Perhaps the Misses Blair would be kind enough to stand by the door of the church, and you too, Brigadier Wessex. We won't ask you to go outside, ladies. Nor you either for the moment, Brigadier,' Whitelaw said. 'But pretend you've just come in. Lights out, please, Sergeant Donaldson.'

There was some argument between the sisters as to exactly where they had been standing when Wessex arrived, but Whitelaw was patient. In fact he was happy to waste time. Then he made them all go through the motions of their arrivals and their reactions, first to the dark church, then to the lights, and was about to do it again when there was a sharp knock on the door.

'What's that?' Wessex demanded.

'Nothing important,' Whitelaw said; he knew it was the warning from the WPC stationed outside. 'I think we've proved, Brigadier, that you did see the church door closing after someone's departure. You admitted to not being sure before. Would you, please, put on your raincoat, go down the street a few yards and then come back in?'

Wessex grunted. He was far from being a stupid man, and he knew he was being manipulated. He didn't underrate the intelligence of either Tansey or Whitelaw. But he could scarcely object when everyone was waiting for him to do the inspector's bidding. Reluctantly he went, to return minutes later, followed by the WPC and Constable Postgate, who had been to the Pomme d'Or.

'Your cake, sir,' he said, handing the box to Superintendent Tansey.

'Thank you very much,' Tansey said, without a flicker of amusement; he had seen Abbot making a careful note of the time. 'Come and sit down with me. I want to ask you a couple of questions.'

Carefully avoiding the gaze of Sergeant Donaldson, Constable Postgate followed Tansey to a pew in a side aisle. This was something to tell his chums, young Syd Postgate in conference with the great Superintendent Tansey. He had no idea that Tansey, who didn't want to lead him, was having difficulty in framing his questions.

'Constable, I'd like you to retrace in your mind what you have just done. You walked, as instructed, down the street, came back past St Stephen's and went on to the Pomme d'Or. While you were near the church did you notice anyone leaving, anyone at all?'

'Sure, sir! A guy in a raincoat came out. He went ahead of me and turned down the lane. I couldn't see who it was.' Postgate looked around the church; he was growing in confidence every minute. 'It were dark, sir, and he were no more than a thick shadow.'

'As it was on the evening Father Le Merle was killed,' Tansey said, more for his own benefit than for that of the constable. 'This part of Colombury is badly lit. But you found your way to the Pomme d'Or and collected the cake. Incidentally, it's yours if you'd like it.'

'Yes, indeedy. Thank *you*, sir.' And before Tansey could form the next question, he answered it. 'I saw the same guy go back into the church as I was coming along the street just now.'

'The same man? Are you sure?'

Syd Postgate hesitated. 'I assumed he was the same, sir, and it's odds on he was. But one chap in a raincoat looks very much like another, and I might be wrong.'

It was as near confirmation as Tansey could hope to get that Jason Clark, in spite of his adamant belief that he had seen the same man leaving and returning to the church, *might* have been wrong. Tansey was pleased. He was fully aware that in a court of law his experiment would carry no weight, but it satisfied him.

While the superintendent was talking to Syd Postgate, Whitelaw was arranging another test. He persuaded Lorna Porter to sit, eyes shut, where it was believed Kathy Whitely had sat. Then he had the lights put out again, and gave instructions to Dr Porter and Father Sinclair. Porter came out of the sacristy, opening the door only enough to allow himself to slide through, and walked down the aisle, past Father Sinclair, who produced a dirty rag from under the pew and waved it as Porter went by and past his wife.

Porter was laughing when the lights were turned on again. 'That was a nasty trick, Inspector. For a moment I really thought it was Alfred Yorke sitting there. It smelt just like him.'

Whitelaw tried to look apologetic. 'Sorry, Doctor. I'm trying to test how much people notice in the dark. It's quite surprising. If you lose one sense, the others tend to become more acute to compensate, so I'm told. So, if you wouldn't mind, let's have another go with a switch of personnel.'

This time there were volunteers, and Whitelaw accepted them though they didn't interest him. But Mrs Porter noticed that the man with the smelly rag passed her twice, which reasonably enough she found confusing. 'He seemed to be going and coming,' she said.

'Once more, please,' Whitelaw said. 'Mrs Wessex, would you take Mrs Porter's place and, let me see, I'd like Father Hanson and Brigadier Wessex and Mr Gough. We'll make this a little more complicated. Lights out, Sergeant Donaldson.'

'Bloody stupid game,' Wessex muttered to Gough as they joined the inspector.

Whitelaw, whose hearing was sharp, caught the remark, and smiled to himself. 'Please put on your raincoat again, sir,' he said. 'We want this to be as realistic as possible.'

Wessex said nothing, but he did as he was asked, and the 'game' went ahead. The brigadier walked quickly down the aisle and past his wife. He was followed by Father Hanson,

131

who waved the smelly rag, then by Gough and finally by Hanson again, who had hurried around the rear of the church to join the procession.

'Well, Mrs Wessex,' said Whitelaw when the lights were on again. He sat himself down beside her. 'What did you make of that?'

'The first one was my husband,' she said without hesitation. 'After him came the smelly one. I don't know who the third was. It wasn't John. And the fourth was smelly too. Poor Alfred Yorke!' She shook her head. 'He infuriated John and a lot of other people. But I can't help feeling sorry for him, and I can't believe he killed Father Le Merle.'

'The man carrying the dirty rag was Father Hanson,' Whitelaw said, 'and Mr Gough was the man in the middle. You had no idea?'

'No, none, Inspector. It could have been the other way round as far as I was concerned.' She grinned at him. 'I kept my eyes shut and I didn't cheat.'

'I'm sure you didn't, Mrs Wessex,' said Tansey, who had joined them. 'But, tell me, how did you know that the first man to go by was your husband? Intuition?'

'Certainly not, Superintendent. I smelt him.'

'What?'

Tansey and Whitelaw exchanged glances, and Tansey said, 'I'm afraid you'll have to explain that, Mrs Wessex.'

'Simple, Superintendent. I'm familiar with the aftershave lotion that John uses. He's been using the same brand since we were married and, though it's nothing out of the ordinary, I recognized it.'

'Congratulations, Mrs Wessex,' Tansey said. 'You've put us both to shame. I think we'll call it a day – or rather an evening.' And to himself he added, a pretty satisfactory one.

While all this was taking place in the church of St Stephen, Mr Ritchie and Dr Quentin left the hospital together. They knew each other well and, in spite of their age difference, could be described as friends. Lance Ritchie had been a medical student with Peter Quentin's father, and had later encouraged the young man to specialize in the hope of becoming a consultant, rather than settling for general practice.

They said good night. Ritchie added that Quentin must come and have dinner with him very soon; he would speak to his wife. He then started towards the car park. Quentin turned down the path that led to the nurses' home.

It was dark along by the hospital. In spite of Kathy Whitely's murder no extra lighting had yet been installed. Quentin concentrated his thoughts on the weekend to come. On the Saturday morning there was to be a memorial service for Father Le Merle, which he would be duty-bound to attend. But he could leave Colombury immediately afterwards, and be in London in time for a late lunch. He would be glad to get away, even for a couple of days.

Lost in thought, Quentin was startled when a large figure suddenly loomed up in front of him. It was a second before he realized who it was, and his hesitation gave Alfred Yorke his chance. Yorke shouldered Quentin aside with surprising strength, so that the doctor stumbled and nearly fell. Then he ran.

Quentin was quick to recover, but Yorke had a good start and there was every chance he would escape – a thought which angered Quentin. But he could see Ritchie, who was not far from the entrance to the lane, though moving steadily away, and he shouted, 'Stop him! Stop him!'

Ritchie turned. He had no idea what had happened, or who the man dashing headlong towards him was. His immediate thought was that it was a thief who had somehow picked Peter Quentin's pocket or stolen something from him. Alfred Yorke was little more than a name to him.

He acted instinctively. In middle age he was fit, and as a medical student he had been a keen rugby player. Unlike Quentin, he wasn't taken by surprise. He ran back to intercept his quarry and, foiling Yorke's attempt to dodge, he pinioned his arms; his mind registered how thin they were before Yorke seemed to relax, to grow limp.

Quentin reached them. 'Good! You've got him. You know who he is, don't you? It's Alfred Yorke, wanted by the police.'

'Really?'

Pleased with themselves and their capture, the two men were caught off guard. They hadn't expected any further resistance from Yorke. But, without warning, he suddenly kicked backwards, his shoe making a satisfactory contact with Ritchie's leg. Simultaneously he wrenched himself free and punched Quentin in the stomach. Both his captors were momentarily incapacitated. Ritchie cried out and staggered off the path to fall heavily into the bushes. Quentin doubled up, fighting against an almost overwhelming desire to vomit.

By the time Quentin had recovered, helped Ritchie to stand, and assured himself that the older man was all right, there was no sign of Alfred Yorke.

CHAPTER 15

Angela Cross sat at her kitchen table and poured herself a second cup of coffee. It was 9.30 in the morning. She had slept badly and had woken with a headache. Bernard had brought her some early morning tea and had told her she should stay in bed; he would get his own breakfast. But she couldn't rest, and as soon as he had gone off to the hospital she had got up, showered and dressed. She was worried.

She knew it was stupid, but she couldn't help it. She wished she had not promised Inspector Whitelaw that if Freddie did come to her she would give him up to the police. She didn't believe she could do it.

Once, many years ago, she had imagined herself in love with Freddie. It would never have worked. She knew that now, and she didn't regret it. The Alfred Yorke of the present day was a very different man from the Freddie she had known then, but all the same she couldn't betray him.

The telephone rang and she went to answer it. The caller was Deirdre Wessex, eager to tell her about what had happened at St Stephen's church the previous evening. It took some while. When she returned to the kitchen Alfred Yorke was sitting at the table, facing her. He was dirty, unshaven, and he smelt. He was also hollow-eyed and his yellowy skin had a pale sheen of sweat on it. He looked desperately ill, and she felt for him.

'Hello, Angie,' he said, his voice hoarse. 'Sorry to intrude on you like this. I spent the night in your garden shed, which is cold and rather damp, and I don't feel my best this morning.'

Angela Cross sat across the table from him. At that distance she could smell him more strongly. 'You need a bath,' she said.

'I need food more. I haven't eaten since I left . . .'

'Left where? Where have you been, Freddie?'

'Here and there, partly in Oxford, doing some research.'

'What research?' She was afraid and she was scornful. 'You know the police are looking for you?'

'Oh yes. I've heard their messages on the radio, and while you were on the phone just now I was reading the *Courier*, all this stuff about a musty smell. In this great town of Colombury, who else smells except me? It's a black joke.' He started to laugh and ended coughing violently.

'Freddie, I have to ask. Did you . . . did you . . .'

'No, I did not, if you mean did I kill Father Le Merle or the girl. Father Le Merle was my friend. He knew about me. I told him everything and he understood. If I could have died instead of him I would have done so, gladly. As for the girl, poor dear, she wasn't important.'

'Not important? How can you say that?'

'She was killed because Father Le Merle's murderer believed she could bear witness against him. She was a danger to him. The police know that perfectly well, though for some reason they tried to confuse the issue by saying she hadn't been in the church. Now they say fresh evidence proves she was there.'

'But why didn't he try to kill you, too?'

'I wasn't around and by the time I returned and gave the police what evidence I had, he must have thought me harmless. How wrong he was!'

'Freddie, Freddie, do you – do you know who the killer is, because you –'

'Angie,' he interrupted her, 'if you want to call the police, call them, the sooner the better. At least they'll give me a cup of tea and a sandwich.'

'I'm sorry,' she said. 'I'm so sorry. What would you like?'

'Anything. Bread and cheese, and something hot to drink.'

Angela Cross was on her feet. Her mind was spinning like a top, and she had to force herself to concentrate. Food was the first essential; moral problems could be considered later.

The coffee in the pot was still hot. She poured Freddie a cup, and made him a ham sandwich. She couldn't help but be shocked by the way he stuffed the food into his mouth and wiped the dribble from his chin with a dirty finger.

'Go and have a bath,' she said. 'It's the second door on the left upstairs. Put your clothes outside the door. I'll wash them, and do what I can with them. I'll leave you a dressing-gown until I can look for some of Bernard's things. Then you can use those temporarily.'

Alfred Yorke gave her a long, hard stare, and then let it soften. 'You won't call the police while I'm in the bathroom? Cross your heart and hope to die, Angie?'

The childish expression took her back more years than she cared to remember. 'Cross my heart and hope to die,' she repeated, her voice thick with unshed tears. 'Meanwhile I'll find you something to wear and ... and cook you a hot meal.'

Half an hour later, Alfred Yorke returned to the kitchen. He sniffed appreciatively. Angela Cross was cooking eggs, bacon, sausages, fried potatoes and tomatoes, and she had made some fresh coffee. She laughed when she saw him.

Yorke was wearing pyjamas and a dressing-gown belonging to Bernard Cross. Cross was a smaller man, and Yorke's thin arms and legs stuck out from trousers and sleeves. But he had had a long soak in the bath. He had scrubbed his hands and feet. He had washed his hair and shaved, and he looked a different man, though still far from well. He had another coughing fit.

'Here you are,' Angela said, putting a plate in front of him. 'Eat slowly, Freddie. It's bad for you to wolf it down. And there's no hurry. Luckily my cleaning lady doesn't come today, or the gardener, so we won't be interrupted. Bernard won't be home until late this afternoon.'

'I shall be gone long before then,' Yorke said, beginning to eat. 'This is good.'

Angela yearned to ask him where he intended to go, but managed to bite her tongue. 'I've put your clothes in the washing machine, and I've found some of Bernard's that

137

may be useful to you; they're on the bed in the guest room.'

'Thanks, Angie, and thanks for the food. It's great and I needed it.'

She poured them both some coffee and again sat down opposite him. She watched him finish his meal. Her feelings were mixed. There was so much she wanted to ask him, but she doubted if he would trust her with any answers. Nevertheless, she knew she had to try. She waited until Yorke put down his knife and fork.

'Freddie, you were in the church that Saturday night. What happened?'

'Yes, I was there,' Yorke sighed, 'and I've told the police all I saw or heard. It was very little and no help to them. I had been asleep. I woke up and sneezed and the killer went past me.'

'And that's all?'

Yorke nodded, and Angela suddenly had the impression that there was more, but that he had no intention of telling her – or anyone. Why? she asked herself. Freddie, who had appeared to be an extrovert, had always been a little secretive.

'Then why not give yourself up to them? Answer whatever they want to ask?'

'Because they'll merely lock me up and I don't intend to spend my last – the last years of my life in prison. I don't trust them, Angie. They need to find a culprit and I seem to have been nominated. After all, I've got a record, don't forget. It would be easy to make a case against me.'

'I don't believe they'd do that, not the men who are in charge of this case.' She remembered her tea with Whitelaw, and grew silent.

'Is there any more coffee?' Yorke asked.

'Sure. And I must go and look at your washing.'

It was safer to keep to practical things, she thought as she went into the utility room. She would do what she could to help Freddie, but it was useless to argue with him; he would do whatever he wanted.

*   *   *

138

'There seems no doubt that Yorke is in the district,' Tansey said. 'He was twice sighted in Oxford, by the librarian and by Gemma Drayton, and there was that encounter yesterday evening in the hospital grounds with the two doctors.'

'A pity they couldn't hold him,' Whitelaw said. 'I'd have thought Quentin would have been strong enough to cope even if Ritchie wasn't.'

'Yorke's not a simple man to deal with in any respect.' Tansey shrugged. 'Certainly the police don't have much luck with him.'

The superintendent and his inspector were having lunch together at headquarters. The mess was three-quarters empty and, having chosen an isolated corner table, they knew they wouldn't be disturbed. They were discussing the events of the previous evening.

'It's ironic that there he was, almost within our grasp, and we were going up and down the aisle at St Stephen's – not personally, of course – waving a dirty rag,' Whitelaw said.

'It wasn't an altogether useless exercise,' Tansey pointed out. 'We know that the killer, had he so wished, had time to commit his crime, leave the church, rid himself of the knife, find a temporary hiding place for the chalice – though I admit I haven't seen a likely place for that – until he could retrieve it, and finally return to the church.'

'A scenario like that would fit either Yorke or Wessex.'

'Yes. But Yorke had no known motive. Wessex had a motive in that he had a running quarrel with Le Merle about Yorke – a quarrel which seems to have amounted to a kind of obsession.'

'That's pretty weak as a motive for murder, sir,' said Whitelaw.

'I agree. There's also the point that Kathy Whitely gave no indication to her boyfriend, Brian Minton, that the man with the musty smell had passed her twice, which tells against it being Yorke. On the other hand, according to his wife, who should know and wasn't lying, Wessex always uses an aftershave which no one could describe as musty. And, to sum up, for all his assurance, Jason Clark, as PC Postgate has shown, could easily have been wrong in stating that the man he saw going into the church, whom we know to have been Wessex, was the same man he saw leaving the place earlier.'

'So they're both exonerated, and we're left with person or persons unknown once more,' Whitelaw said.

'Yes,' Tansey agreed. 'In my opinion the field is wide open. We'll have to start again and dig deeper. The problem is where to start digging. But one thing's for sure – we won't solve the case by sitting here over our coffee. Let's go.'

They had almost reached the superintendent's office when his secretary burst out of her outer room into the corridor. 'Superintendent! Oh, Superintendent, I'm so glad I've found you.'

'What is it?' Tansey asked calmly. His secretary was a competent, self-contained woman, not given to over-reacting, but she was clearly upset now. 'What is it?' he repeated, this time more urgently.

'There was a phone call. The lady said her name was Angela Cross and it was important she should speak to you. I was about to say that you were not in your office at present when she screamed, and either she or someone else slammed down the receiver.'

Tansey and Whitelaw exchanged glances. 'Yorke?' Tansey said.

'Probably,' Whitelaw agreed. 'Shall I go?'

'We'll both go,' Tansey said, and added to his secretary, 'If I'm wanted, I'm on my way to Colombury and can be contacted on the mobile phone. Don't mention Mrs Cross.'

'Right, sir,' she said.

'You drive,' Tansey said to Whitelaw as they approached the car. 'I'll try Mrs Cross's number.'

They could hear the phone ringing, but there was no answer and Whitelaw, who knew Angela Cross better than Tansey, was anxious. 'Sir, shouldn't we get Sergeant Donaldson to go directly to the house with some of his minions?' he asked tentatively.

'No, I think not.' Tansey spoke with assurance. 'At the rate you're driving, we'll be there almost as soon. It's possible, if it is Yorke, that he's shut himself up with her, and I wouldn't trust Donaldson in a tricky siege or hostage situation. Alternatively, Yorke may have shut her up where she can't reach a phone and departed, in which case a brief delay will be no loss.'

'Supposing he's killed her?'

'The same applies. But why should he have killed her? She seems to have been the one member of the family who has been kind and generous to him.'

'Father Le Merle was kind to him, too.'

'But we'd agreed that, contrary to general opinion, the chances are that Yorke didn't kill Le Merle, so why should he risk a murder charge by doing for his cousin?' Tansey sounded slightly irritated.

'It isn't logical, but he could be round the bend.'

'We'll soon find out. Of course, you know where we're going. You know where the Crosses live?'

'Yes, sir. It's close to the Pettigrews' house; that's the place where the chalice was eventually found in the garden.'

'Interesting,' Tansey said, and lapsed into silence.

It was a pleasant, square house, built of the familiar Cotswold stone, not as big as some of its neighbours, but what an estate agent would describe as a 'desirable property'. It looked solid and comfortable, without being pretentious.

'I'll try the front door. You go round the back,' Tansey said. 'If he's still there he may have heard the car and be leaving through the garden.'

To Whitelaw's relief, for he had no desire for a chase, there was no sign of Yorke at the rear of the house, and he found the back door unlocked. It led into a small hall, and then to a kitchen. Everything was quiet except for a dripping tap.

'Mrs Cross!' he called. 'Are you there, Mrs Cross?'

'I'm in here, in the sitting room,' came the reply.

Whitelaw raced. He could hear the front door bell and registered that Tansey had his thumb on it. The sitting room was the second door he tried.

Angela Cross was sitting in an upright chair, shielded from view from the window. She was not gagged, but she was

141

bound, wrists and ankles, by what Whitelaw later discovered to be a clothes line, and unable to move.

'Are you all right?' he asked immediately.

'Yes, just uncomfortable. I'm glad you've come. I thought I might have to wait for Bernard.' She managed to smile.

'Great!' Whitelaw said, thankful she was apparently unharmed and in reasonably good spirits. 'I'll just let Superintendent Tansey in and then get something to cut you free. Won't be a minute.'

It was a little longer than that before Angela Cross was free and rubbing her wrists and ankles. She was pale but composed, and clearly hadn't suffered too badly from her experience. She refused tea and asked for a whisky, which Whitelaw poured for her.

'Now, Mrs Cross,' Tansey said, sitting himself opposite her. 'You insist you don't need to see a doctor. So please tell us what happened. Your cousin, Alfred Yorke, has been here?'

Angela nodded. 'I went to answer the phone, and when I came back I found Freddie sitting calmly at the kitchen table. He was dirty. He smelt. But above all he looked desperately ill, close to exhaustion. He said he'd spent the night in our garden shed and he hadn't eaten for ages. I gave him a ham sandwich and coffee, and while he had a bath I –'

'You could have phoned us then,' Tansey interrupted.

Angela Cross bit her lip. She couldn't tell them about the old childish tag: 'Cross my heart and hope to die.' They wouldn't understand. They would think her a fool – but she and Freddie . . . 'I couldn't,' she said. 'I just couldn't.' Without warning she burst into tears.

'It's all right, Mrs Cross,' Tansey said consolingly. 'It doesn't matter. You didn't telephone us then. Go on from there. What happened next?'

'I cooked him a hot meal, washed his clothes, found him some of Bernard's, including a raincoat. His was torn. Gave him money, not much, twenty-five pounds, which was all I had. I'd planned to go to the bank this afternoon. Then – then he asked me if I could give him some writing-paper and a stamp.'

'Writing-paper and a stamp?' Tansey was disbelieving.

142

'I thought it odd, but it was only to get me out of the way. When I came back, Freddie had gone – or I thought he had.'

'And this was when you decided to phone us, Mrs Cross?'

'No, not even then,' she said drily. 'I couldn't do it – I know I gave Inspector Whitelaw my word, but when it came to it, I couldn't. I'm sorry. I just couldn't betray Freddie.'

'But you did, Mrs Cross. You did phone us at last.' Tansey pressed her.

'When I discovered he had stolen the knife. I was afraid then for him and – I don't know. He'd said or implied some peculiar things.'

'Take it easy, Mrs Cross. First, what knife?'

'A very sharp carving knife. Bernard's favourite. I'd used it to cut some ham for Freddie and left it on the draining board. Freddie knew I'd miss it and would probably phone you, so he didn't leave the house as I'd thought. He waited in the coats cupboard and when I did try to phone from the hall he came out, forced me into the sitting room and tied me up.'

'Did he threaten you?' Whitelaw asked.

Angela Cross shook her head. 'No, he was very gentle. He wouldn't hurt me, but it would have been a long wait for Bernard if you hadn't come.'

Tansey and Whitelaw exchanged wordless glances again. It was clear to them that Mrs Cross still had faith in her Freddie, but the fact that he was now armed with a sharp knife boded no good for someone. The last thing either of them wanted was another killing.

'Mrs Cross,' Tansey said, 'what did you mean by saying that Yorke had said or implied some peculiar things?'

'When I asked him where he had been he said, "Here and there and doing some research in Oxford", which sounded mad. Then he denied killing Father Le Merle – and I believe him – but I got the impression that he knew or suspected who the culprit was. He said that the man – Father Le Merle's murderer – thought that he, Freddie, was harmless, which was why he hadn't tried to kill him as he had killed that nurse. But he was wrong, Freddie said. He said something obscure about a black joke, too, something to do with him

– he meant himself – smelling because he didn't wash much, but I didn't understand it.'

Angela Cross shook her head wearily. She was finally exhausted. Her headache had returned, and she wished the two men would stop asking questions and go. She had had enough.

Tansey was perceptive. He said, 'Mrs Cross, I'm going to phone your husband and ask him to come home.' He would also have to issue a general warning that Alfred Yorke was now armed and probably dangerous, but there was no need to tell her that. 'Meanwhile, Inspector Whitelaw, with your permission, will have a quick look round the house and garden to make sure Yorke has really gone, and I suggest you go and lie down. You've had a shock, though fortunately there's no great harm done. We'll lock up and wait outside in the car until your husband comes. We'll also arrange to keep a man on duty outside for a few days.'

'Thank you, Superintendent – Inspector,' she said. 'Thank you both very much, but I don't have to be guarded. Freddie would never hurt me.'

'No, Mrs Cross,' Tansey said and thought, as he knew Whitelaw was also thinking, of famous last words.

CHAPTER 16

Alfred Yorke was cold and wet and miserable. His plans, such as they were, had gone awry. Ever since he had left the Crosses' house the previous afternoon, everything had come apart. The sky had clouded over and a thin sticky drizzle had started to fall. He wouldn't have minded this too much, although it was uncomfortable; to some extent it suited his purpose. But much sooner than he expected he had become aware that he was being hunted.

He had moved from one hiding place to another, only to be forced to accept that a thorough search of Colombury and the surrounding district was in progress. He hadn't expected Superintendent Tansey to act with such speed or to show such efficiency. Clearly, police from stations other than the local one had been drafted in. He almost wished that he hadn't stolen the knife, since he realized that now, known to be armed, he was considered a dangerous criminal. The idea amused him; for once, he thought, they were right.

He had had two narrow escapes. Once he had been cornered in a narrow alley, which had proved to be a dead end, and he had just managed to climb over a wall into a builder's yard and get through into another street. Then, almost immediately, he had been confronted by a second crisis as two police officers came towards him. On this occasion he had dived into the nearest shop, and only when the scent of flowers hit him did he realize where he was. He had busied himself filling in the card that the florist had provided – he hoped Angie would enjoy the expensive arrangement for which she was in effect paying – while the officers lingered outside for a moment before slowly passing on their way.

He had been sweating – he couldn't help himself – but the florist failed to notice.

He had been thankful when it grew dark, though the drizzle had turned to a steady rain. Carefully he made his way towards the hospital, but there were even more police here, and bright lights. He had retreated, instinctively, to St Stephen's church, but that too seemed to be guarded. Frustrated, he had nearly abandoned his quest and walked into the police station and announced himself to Sergeant Donaldson, but the thought of his unfulfilled purpose and the triumph he would see on Donaldson's foxy face had dissuaded him. Slowly, because he was feeling far from well, he had set off across the fields to the woods where he knew that, unless they used sniffer dogs, they would never find his hide.

At least it had been dry there and not too cold, but he had slept badly. His cough had kept him awake. It was a relief when dawn came, though it was still raining, a grey, depressing day. He made for Colombury and the hospital. He knew this was his last chance; if he failed this morning he might get away from the district but there would be no coming back and, if he failed and was unlucky, he would end up in prison with nothing achieved or likely to be achieved. As he trudged along through the fields, he told himself that the one thing he must not do was fear failure. If he got half a chance he would succeed.

Approaching the town he grew wary, aware that the police wouldn't have stopped looking for him because another day had dawned. On the contrary, having done their best to check that he hadn't left the area, they would be more eager to catch him. However, it was still very early and, apart from a milk float and a couple of workmen who, to judge from the scrap of their conversation that he had overheard, were coming off a night shift, he saw no one until he reached the hospital grounds. Colombury was not yet awake.

He hid in the bushes near the nurses' home. He needed to spy out the land with some care. There was a police officer in front of the main door as he had expected, and he was about to move parallel to the path that led to the hospital entrance when another officer appeared from that direction with a German shepherd dog on a chain lead. Yorke froze.

The two officers, taking shelter in the doorway, chatted amiably while the dog sprawled at their feet. Then, glancing surreptitiously around they lit cigarettes. Yorke grinned to himself; unless the dog had been following a clearly defined trail – which was obviously not the case – the cigarette smoke should deaden its powers for a few moments. He began to move slowly and cautiously, aware that dogs were conscious of movement in the earth as well as scents. He was not interested in the nurses' home as such. His objective was the car park of the senior hospital staff.

'I think it's absolutely absurd,' Rhoda Ritchie said. 'If people want to have a memorial service for Father Le Merle on Saturday, let them have it, but there's no reason for you to be there, Lance, when it means ruining one of your free weekends. We had agreed to go to London. This place is only possible if you can get away from it at frequent intervals.'

Lance Ritchie continued to butter his toast and didn't answer. The Ritchies were having an argument over breakfast. Rhoda had been looking forward to a long weekend in London, shopping, going to the theatre, visiting old friends. She couldn't understand her husband's determination to attend a memorial service for a man he hadn't known and who hadn't even been a member of the hospital staff.

'All the other consultants are going, and those junior doctors who aren't on duty,' he said at last. 'I have to show some *esprit de corps*, Rhoda. We can leave for London after the service.'

'If we can't go on Friday afternoon it's not worth the effort,' she said obstinately. 'As for *esprit de corps*, that's a load of rubbish. You didn't go to that nurse's funeral.'

'That was different.'

'How?'

'She was not one of my nurses. I doubt if I'd spoken more than half a dozen words to her and – and – Don't you understand that Father Le Merle was something of a celebrity in Colombury?'

'You mean like Alfred Yorke?'

The argument continued until Ritchie left for the hospital, and was the more bitter because it was unnecessary. He did not really need to attend the memorial service for Le Merle. He didn't want to attend it and listen to a heap of twaddle about what a good man the wretched priest had been. So why was he determined to go?

Because – when he could bring himself to face the answer – it was essential he should fit in, make a success of this job, for which he had had to compete with a surprising number of other candidates. Now he was here it should have been easy for him in an unimportant hospital in a small town, but it wasn't. No one doubted his skills, but they seemed to judge him as a person, and of course Rhoda's attitude to the other women she had met had not helped. Nevertheless, it was not altogether her fault, Lance Ritchie thought; it was just bloody bad luck, a chance in a million, that after all these years he should run into Paul Le Merle again.

He had reached the car park, where he slid his Jaguar into the slot reserved for him. He still had to walk, rain or fine, a few hundred yards to the hospital entrance, and he recalled with regret the chauffeur-driven car that had for a time been one of his perks in London.

Reluctantly he got out of his seat, locked the car and, head bent and shoulders hunched although the rain had ceased, started to walk. He was early; he had been glad to get away from Rhoda. But a short distance ahead of him he saw Bernard Cross and Peter Quentin with a couple of nurses in front of them. He lengthened his stride.

The attack came as a complete surprise. One moment he sensed someone behind him and half turned to say good morning. The next moment he was flung to the ground and he felt a searing pain as a knife was thrust into his side and, it seemed to him, was twisted and withdrawn. He didn't wait for the second blow that he knew was threatened. He seized the wrist of his attacker and, using all his ebbing strength, forced the knife point away from himself. Then, as he heard the wrist snap, he pushed the knife deep into Alfred Yorke's chest.

Bernard Cross said, 'I saw it happen, Superintendent. I saw it with my own eyes.'

Tempted to ask how else he could have seen it, Tansey suppressed a smile. Cross was in a state of mild shock. He had come to the hospital this morning only because Angela had insisted; after the events of the previous day he had hated to leave her, conscious that Alfred Yorke, armed with a killing knife, was still at large, and now he was sure he ought not to have left her, though with Yorke about to go into surgery the danger was surely past. He wondered how she would take the news about Yorke; she had remained convinced that he was harmless.

Suddenly aware that he had been silent for some while and that the superintendent was waiting for him to continue, he said, 'I was walking from the car park with Peter Quentin and we were almost at the entrance to the hospital when I glanced over my shoulder. I saw Ritchie and obviously he had seen us. I hesitated, wondering if I should wait for him to catch us up. He's the sort of man who expects little courtesies like that; in fact, he seems to be a touchy character and it's easy to offend him.' Cross stopped. 'I shouldn't be saying these things about him when the poor devil's in such a bad way.'

'Mr Cross,' Tansey intervened; he was growing impatient. 'Please go on. You saw Mr Ritchie approaching?'

'Yes. Sorry,' Cross said. 'I don't usually waffle so much, Superintendent. Ritchie was about a hundred yards away when Yorke leapt on him from behind. I think he must have knifed him at the same time. Anyhow, they both fell to the ground and struggled for the knife. Fortunately – though don't tell Angela I said so – Ritchie managed to hold his own and stick the knife into Yorke. When Quentin reached them – he's younger than me and quicker – they had rolled apart and were lying there. They were almost unconscious. As Quentin will tell you when he's free, Ritchie apparently managed to say, "He tried to kill me." Ritchie sounded surprised, according to Quentin.'

'Why shouldn't he be surprised?' Tansey said. 'Ritchie didn't know Yorke. He told me he hadn't come across him before the other night when he and Quentin nearly caught him.'

'Yorke must be mad,' Cross added absently. 'When I think of yesterday and Angela . . . It makes one believe in God. At least Yorke's not likely to kill anyone else now.'

'You mean he's dead?'

'No, not yet, but I gather there's not a great deal of hope, although the hospital will do its best, of course.'

'They damn well better had,' Tansey said with such force that Cross stared at him, and he added, 'Mr Cross, in 95 per cent of criminal cases the obvious is the answer, but in the other 5 per cent this is not true. Yorke must get the best possible treatment – and so, it goes without saying, must Mr Ritchie. How is he?'

'Superintendent, I'm not a doctor. I can only accept what I'm told,' Cross said coldly. 'Mr Ritchie's condition is serious. The knife wound did horrible things to his gut, but he's not in immediate danger of death, according to the prognosis. We have, however, taken the precaution of sending for his wife, though there's not much she can do for him at present.'

'And Alfred Yorke's relations? Have you told your wife, Mr Cross?'

'Not yet, Superintendent.' Cross's smile was wry.

'Then I suggest you do, Mr Cross, before she hears of it from someone else. I'll go and see if Dr Quentin is free.'

Having decided that there was nothing more he could do in Colombury at the moment, Superintendent Tansey had returned to headquarters. He felt tense and vaguely aggrieved, though he could have produced no logical reason for such feelings. The Chief Constable, who considered that the case was now wrapped up apart from a few formalities, was satisfied and obviously didn't care whether Yorke lived or died.

Tansey, however, did care, and he was not satisfied. There

was something wrong, something he had missed, some anomaly, and it irked him that he couldn't put his finger on it. For his own peace of mind he needed to know what it was. He shook his head. He must do his best to set his brain to work, and consider every aspect of the affair again.

On the face of it, the case against Alfred Yorke was proven without doubt. Quentin had confirmed Cross's evidence in every respect. They would both be prepared to swear on oath that Ritchie was hurrying to join them when without warning he had been attacked from behind by Alfred Yorke. Only the fact that Ritchie was a strong and healthy man had saved him; he had been able to overcome what appeared to be a maniacal attack from a much weaker, almost certainly sick man. Quentin was sure that he would never have reached the struggling men in time to save Ritchie if their respective strengths had been reversed. So, although Yorke was the one likely to die, Ritchie was in the clear and, on the basis of the other doctors' evidence, no blame could be attached to him.

And, if Yorke did survive and come to trial, Angela Cross would be forced to testify that he had stolen the knife from her house the day before the attack on Ritchie. It implied premeditation. But why should Alfred Yorke have wanted to kill Lance Ritchie? What was his motive? It had all the appearance of a motiveless attempt, similar in that respect to the killing of Father Le Merle, and it didn't make sense. Superintendent Tansey liked things to make sense. He decided to abandon his tortuous thoughts, and go home to his wife and family – and sanity.

CHAPTER 17

At 2 o'clock on Friday morning the young nurse who was monitoring Alfred Yorke in the intensive care unit of the hospital noted a change in him. He had survived an operation the previous day, but he was very weak and she had been warned he might not last the night. Now he had become restless, his eyes were open and he seemed to be trying to say something. She watched him anxiously for a minute before going to stand beside his bed. She leant over him.

'A priest, please. Fetch me a priest,' he whispered.

'Yes. All right,' she promised, and was glad to see him relax.

But the sister in charge of the unit demurred. It was the middle of the night. It wasn't fair to rouse a priest from his sleep and expect him to come to the hospital merely because a wicked old man wanted to confess his sins before he died.

'Father Le Merle would have come, Sister,' the young nurse said. 'He once spent an entire night holding a frightened man's hand, and the chap wasn't even a Catholic.'

'Well, Father Le Merle isn't with us any more, thanks to your patient – and neither is Nurse Whitely.'

'We don't know for sure –'

'We know for sure that he did his best to kill poor Mr Ritchie. But if you want to phone St Stephen's presbytery, you're welcome. Only don't blame me if Father Hanson or the new priest gives you a flea in your ear.'

'Mr Yorke could be dead by morning.'

'So – go ahead.' Owing to a shortage of staff the sister had been on night duty for two shifts, and they had been fraught nights; she wasn't feeling her best. 'Go ahead,' she urged, as her junior hesitated. 'Phone! No one will come.'

*　　　*　　　*

Father Hanson nearly proved the sister right. He woke slowly and, tempted to put his head under the pillow, answered the ringing only because he was afraid the continuing noise might wake Father Sinclair, who was sleeping in the spare room next to him. He was horrified to see the time. He listened to the nurse's request with irritation and was about to refuse to go to the hospital until morning, when she mentioned Father Le Merle.

He would have liked to have replied that he was not a saint like Father Le Merle, but the memory of the late priest stayed him. Instead he surprised himself by saying, 'Right. I'll be along as soon as I can.'

He got out of bed and dressed hurriedly, shivering in the cold room. He had a busy day ahead of him and could have done with a good night's sleep, but there was no hope of that now. As he reached for the case that contained all he would need to perform the last rites for a dying man, he wondered whether he should make himself a hot drink before leaving the presbytery. Reluctantly he decided against it. The nurse had sounded urgent, and he didn't want to arrive to find Yorke dead, his effort wasted.

He decided to walk to the hospital; it would be as quick as getting out the car, then having to park it, and, with Yorke safely in intensive care, there was no longer any fear of being attacked. He thought of Father Le Merle, of Nurse Whitely, of the consultant, Lance Ritchie. Yorke's attacks on them had neither rhyme nor reason. The man was mad. Even if he came to trial, his barrister would plead diminished responsibility, but there didn't seem much chance that the case would come to court. The nurse had implied that Yorke was very near death.

Indeed, as he pulled up his chair beside the bed and looked down at the waxen face on the pillow, he could easily have believed that the man lying there was already dead. Then Alfred Yorke suddenly opened his eyes and focused.

'Cross yourself,' Father Hanson said, 'and do your best to make a good confession, Mr Yorke. Believe that soon you will be ... be ...' He stumbled over the word 'judged' and replaced it by 'with God', but he couldn't bring himself to call

153

this murderer 'my son'. 'You understand what I'm saying, Mr Yorke?'

'Perfectly, Father Hanson.' The voice was weak, but full of purpose. 'I will make my confession later. First, listen carefully to what I have to say, please, and don't interrupt. I haven't much strength. Even if this hadn't happened I wouldn't have had much longer to live. I've an inoperable cancer, as my postmortem will show, which is why I determined to kill Ritchie. However, it seems I have failed, so . . .'

Hanson listened; it was his duty as a priest. Twice he tried to interrupt, but Yorke paid him no attention, and continued with his absurd, incredible story. Hanson decided not to interrupt again. The man was mad, deranged, and it was best to humour him. But Alfred Yorke didn't sound either mad or deranged, and gradually John Hanson realized that against his will he was half believing him.

'Yes, I promise you, my son,' he said as Yorke came to an end. 'I will tell Superintendent Tansey what you have told me, and it will be up to him to act as he thinks fit.'

'He must act, Father. Impress on him that there is no way I would tell lies on my death bed. I would be too afraid. And justice must be done.' Exhausted, Yorke sank back against the pillows and shut his eyes.

An hour later he died. Father Hanson still sat beside him, holding his hand.

Superintendent Tansey was informed of Alfred Yorke's death as soon as he reached his office that morning. There was also a message from Cross saying that Lance Ritchie had had a good night, and it would be possible to interview him later in the day, though only for a few minutes. This was followed by a telephone call from Father Hanson, who wanted to speak to the superintendent urgently.

'I'll have to go to Colombury,' Tansey said. 'I was hoping to avoid it today. I've a mountain of paperwork, and a report for the Chief Constable.'

'Could I go instead?' Whitelaw asked.

Tansey hesitated, thinking of Ritchie's reputation as a

rather difficult man. 'No. I'll take Abbot and make it very formal. Ritchie may feel badly that we didn't offer him protection after his encounter with Yorke the other evening.'

In the event, he found Lance Ritchie extremely affable and ready to blame himself. 'I feel miserable – dreadful – that the man should have died,' he said. 'But, to be honest, I didn't know what I was doing. My one thought – it was instinct rather than thought – was to defend myself. I assume there won't be any trouble?'

'I shouldn't imagine so, sir.' Tansey was reassuring. 'You may have to give evidence at the inquest if you are well enough, but there are several other witnesses to prove that Yorke's attack on you was completely unprovoked and, what's more, that the man was a stranger to you.'

'He should have been locked up,' Ritchie said. 'Father Le Merle, that little nurse – and it could easily have been me, too. He was insane, of course. Did you know, Superintendent, that he went into a florist's in Colombury on Wednesday, after he had stolen the knife from the Crosses' home and everyone was looking for him, and sent Angela Cross a great bouquet, which I'm sure she deserved after what she's suffered at his hand?'

'No, I didn't know,' Tansey said, and wondered if Mrs Cross had wept when she received the flowers.

A nurse came in at this point to say that Mr Ritchie's doctor was on his rounds, and it was time for the police officers to leave. Tansey went without demur or regret. Lance Ritchie could not have been more pleasant, but there was something about the man he didn't care for – perhaps it had been his somewhat patronizing attitude towards Angela Cross.

'What did you think of him, Abbot?' he asked, as they left the hospital and made their way to St Stephen's church.

'If you want me to be truthful, sir, I thought him too damned self-centred,' Abbot said. 'He's the kind of guy who'd refuse to give someone a lift to save himself from a minor inconvenience.'

Tansey laughed, but he considered this a perceptive remark on Abbot's part.

*   *   *

'I may be wasting your time, Superintendent,' Father Hanson said, 'but I gave my word to a dying man, so I have to keep it.'

'You're referring to Alfred Yorke,' Tansey said, thinking the priest unnecessarily pompous.

Hanson nodded. 'I was called out last night to give him the last rites, as I thought, but he told me an extraordinary tale, and made me promise to relay it to you. At first I didn't believe it, but then I had second, third, fourth and fifth thoughts, and now I think part of it may be true, or at least that Alfred Yorke believed it to be true. You're not a Catholic, are you, Superintendent?'

Wishing that Hanson would come to the point, the superintendent was a little startled by the question. 'No, Father Hanson, I am not,' he said, 'but it is usually accepted by a court that a death-bed statement to a responsible individual (such as yourself) is probably the truth, in the absence of contradictory evidence. Yorke knew he was about to die?'

'Yes, he did and, in spite of his, er, peculiarities, he was a devout Catholic in many ways.' Hanson sighed. 'What I'm trying to say is that I cannot accept that in his situation he would have deliberately lied. On the other hand . . .'

Tansey looked around the uncomfortable, scrupulously clean parlour with its oversized crucifix on one wall, and waited. But Hanson seemed unable to continue, even when Abbot gave an encouraging cough.

At last Tansey said, 'Just repeat to me what Alfred Yorke told you, Father Hanson. Sergeant Abbot will take it down and we will consider its veracity in due course. For the moment we'll accept that Yorke believed what he was saying.'

'All right,' Hanson agreed. 'I'll do my best. But you must remember that he rambled a good deal – after all, he was very ill – and sometimes I may not have heard him correctly. He said some odd things.'

'Just go ahead, Father Hanson.' Tansey recalled that Angela Cross had said much the same of some of Yorke's remarks. 'Take your time.'

'First, he strongly denied that he had killed Father Le

Merle. He had been asleep in the church. He had woken and seen the sacristy door closing. The man who had come out passed close by him, so close he could have touched him.'

Once he had begun, Hanson seemed to have no difficulty in continuing, but he produced nothing that Tansey didn't already know or surmise, except that Yorke had terminal cancer, which suggested that some of the man's mysterious disappearances could be due to sojourns in hospital. However, Hanson's account, which so far had been straightforward, did accord with that of Angela Cross and its consistency told in Yorke's favour.

'Now we come to the tricky bit, Superintendent,' Hanson went on rather apologetically. 'Yorke admitted that he stole the knife from the Crosses' house *with the express intention* of killing Mr Ritchie. He said that he himself had only a short time to live because of his cancer, and he was determined that justice should be done. I'm afraid he didn't have much faith in the police.'

'I don't follow that,' Tansey said.

'He was certain that Mr Ritchie had killed Father Le Merle and subsequently the nurse.'

'Ritchie?'

'I know, Superintendent. He's the most unlikely suspect. He has only been in Colombury for a month or two, and as far as I know he never even met Le Merle.'

'Did Yorke say why he decided Ritchie was the killer? Did he give any grounds for this belief?'

'Yes. He said he smelt Mr Ritchie as he passed him in the church, and again when they struggled in the hospital grounds last Tuesday evening. It was Mr Ritchie's aftershave lotion which he recognized. It had a strong musky smell. He said the media got it wrong. The smell was musky, not musty.'

'Musk is the basis of many scents, and Ritchie can't be the only man to use a particular brand,' Tansey objected. 'Did Yorke give any other reason for accusing Ritchie? What about motive? Why on earth should Ritchie have wanted Father Le Merle dead?

Father Hanson shook his head. 'He said he didn't know

what Mr Ritchie's motive might have been, though he had done his best to look into it – whatever he meant by that. But he wanted me to impress on you, Superintendent, that he had done all he could, and now it was up to you.'

'Up to me?' Tansey thought of the Chief Constable; Holy Cow would not be interested, since for him the case was closed.

'And now it's up to me,' Superintendent Tansey repeated later in the day, having put Inspector Whitelaw in the picture. 'The problem is, where the hell do I start?'

'You're going to take some action?' Whitelaw was tentative. 'It won't be easy – or popular.'

'I know that. It may even prove impossible, but I must try. After all, we agreed, didn't we, that Alfred Yorke was probably innocent and that a "person unknown" was probably guilty. Now we have Yorke's death-bed statement, which would seem to confirm his innocence.'

'But not Ritchie's guilt.'

'No, definitely not, but a few things can be checked – mostly on the phone.'

'Such as?'

'What time Ritchie arrived at the Crosses' party on the night of Father Le Merle's murder,' Tansey said thoughtfully. 'That could clear him completely. If it can be shown when he left the hospital, he would have had to go home and change and then –'

'Why? Brigadier Wessex planned to go straight to the party from town.'

'Yes, but he had only come into Colombury to see his lawyer. He hadn't been working all day as Ritchie had, although it was a Saturday. Ritchie seems to be a meticulous man. I feel sure he would have showered and changed before going out for the evening.'

Whitelaw grinned. 'I could check on his musky aftershave lotion too.'

'You could ask Brian Minton if he's sure his girlfriend said musty and not musky. That is, if you're with me, Maurice. This could spell trouble, as you implied.'

'I'm with you, Dick. I thought that went without saying.'

'Thanks.'

'What else?'

'That Oxford librarian might come up with something. Yorke told Mrs Cross he'd been doing some research. It's worth a try. And that's it for the moment,' Tansey concluded ruefully. 'I can't think of anything else.'

By the end of the day Inspector Whitelaw had checked everything checkable, but without much in the way of positive results. Angela Cross had recalled her disastrous dinner party in honour of the Ritchies with wry amusement, and volunteered that they had arrived late; but it had been impossible even for the tactful Whitelaw to discover when the gynaecologist had left the hospital that evening. Neither the Oxford librarian, willing though she had been, nor Brian Minton was of any help; the librarian didn't know what Alfred Yorke had been researching, and Minton couldn't be sure whether Kathy had said musty or musky.

Indeed, the one positive result was an expensive bottle of musky strong-smelling aftershave lotion, which was to sit in a drawer of Tansey's desk until in due course it was thrown away.

CHAPTER 18

Superintendent Tansey had expected a large congregation at St Stephen's for the memorial service for Father Le Merle. What he had not expected was that the church would be packed, and certainly not with such a cross-section of Colombury's population. Arriving a little late, he found himself wedged sideways against a pillar in an over-full pew halfway up a side aisle. This, however, had the advantage that he had an excellent view of the church and could observe its occupants without appearing to be over-curious.

Christopher Le Merle, the dead priest's brother, had phoned Tansey earlier in the week to say that he and his family would be in Oxford for the weekend, and would be attending the memorial service in Colombury. He had asked after the progress of the case, but he hadn't pressed. He was a tactful man and was well aware that the media had not been kind to the superintendent or to the Serious Crime Squad of the Thames Valley Police. Tansey now recognized Le Merle's back in the front pew, which had clearly been reserved for the family.

They were no surprise. Nor were the people from the hospital, except for their number. Among them Tansey saw the Crosses with a woman whom he took to be Mrs Ritchie, presumably representing her husband; Peter Quentin, the lapsed Catholic; Steve Poole, the physiotherapist with his exotic girlfriend; Sister Bascombe and a bevy of nurses, including Gemma Drayton. In addition there were Dr and Mrs Porter, Brigadier and Mrs Wessex, Patrick Gough, the Misses Blair and Inspector Whitelaw's in-laws, the Gronskis from the Pomme d'Or restaurant.

Some of the remainder, such as Mat Brown and Jason Clark, Tansey knew slightly, and some by sight from the Windrush Arms, but most of them he didn't recognize. A large group of teenagers in jeans and T-shirts were a surprise; he wouldn't have expected them to be there on a fine Saturday morning. Indeed, he wouldn't have expected half the people there to have given up a free morning for a memorial service for a man they couldn't have known well. Obviously, Father Le Merle had been dearly loved by a great many.

And yet it seemed that someone had hated – or feared – him enough to kill him.

Superintendent Tansey's thoughts wandered as the organist began to play, and the congregation to sing 'Jerusalem', a song which everyone seemed to know, and the two priests, Father Sinclair and Father Hanson, entered. It was a simple service, prayers, another hymn, Father Hanson to read the first lesson, Christopher Le Merle the second. Then Father Sinclair came forward. A hush fell.

'Friends,' he said, 'you are probably surprised that I, who have only been in Colombury for a matter of days, should be speaking to you about Father Le Merle. The truth is that, apart from his family, I have almost certainly known him longer than anyone here. We met many years ago in Rome, where we were both students at the English College, training to be priests. We were much of an age. I had taught before deciding to become a priest, and Paul Le Merle, as he was then, had studied medicine at Oxford and had travelled widely before realizing that he had a vocation. As a result, we had much in common. We became and remained close friends, though we didn't meet very often.'

Superintendent Tansey found himself sitting upright and tensed. He had been trying to relax in his uncomfortable cramped position beside the pillar, while he prepared to listen to what he hoped would be a short, if somewhat boring, eulogy, of the dead priest. He had to admit that he had initially been a little surprised that the task of delivering it had been allocated to Father Sinclair, rather than to Father Hanson, but now Sinclair had his full attention.

The superintendent was mentally kicking himself. He had not been aware that Sinclair had known Le Merle. No one had mentioned it, and it hadn't occurred to him to ask; it should have done. He had known, because Le Merle's brother had told him, that Le Merle had studied medicine at Oxford, but he had forgotten the fact, and it could be extremely important. What did Sinclair know? What had Alfred Yorke discovered in his 'researches' in the Oxford Public Library? Yorke could have been mistaken, jumped to the wrong conclusion, but he could equally well have been on the right track.

'I've been a bloody fool,' Tansey muttered, too low for his neighbour to catch the words, but loud enough to make him turn and stare at the detective.

'You all right?'

'Yes. Sorry.' Tansey recognized the speaker as a local shop-keeper. 'There's not much room here, is there?'

'Not surprising. Father Le Merle was a fine man – and we all want to pay our respects.' He looked suspiciously at Tansey. 'Press, are you?'

'No,' Tansey said, but didn't elaborate.

While he had been distracted by this pointless conversation the eulogy had come to an end. As in a dream, he heard the prayers that followed, the blessing and the final hymn. He stood with everyone else as they sang 'Ave Maria'. He didn't know the words and made no attempt to join in. He was bent on interrogating Father Sinclair.

As soon as the sacristy door had shut behind the two priests and the congregation had started to leave the church, talking quietly among themselves, Tansey hurried after Father Sinclair. He knocked and went into the sacristy.

'Father Sinclair, I'm sorry to bother you, but I need to ask you a few questions.'

'Not now, I hope, Superintendent. Chris Le Merle has very kindly asked me to lunch with the family at the Pomme d'Or before they drive back to Oxford.'

'My queries won't take long, and they could be important,' Tansey said.

162

Sinclair hesitated. He started to shake his head, then changed his mind; there was an urgency about the superintendent's manner. 'All right,' he said. 'Father Hanson, will you tell the Le Merles I've been detained for a few minutes, and I'll meet them at the Pomme d'Or as soon as I can?'

'Yes, of course, Father.'

With a nod to Tansey, Hanson left them. Sinclair drew out two chairs and gestured to Tansey to sit. Tansey looked around the sacristy and wondered how to begin. He wanted information, but without giving away any in return and particularly without leading the witness.

Sinclair misunderstood his inspection. 'You mind talking in here?' he asked. 'The place has been thoroughly cleaned, physically and spiritually. Mrs Faudin gave it a good scrub, and I blessed it. But, if you like, we can go into the church or the presbytery.'

'This will be fine,' Tansey said. 'Father Sinclair, can you tell me why Father Le Merle decided to become a priest?'

Sinclair shrugged. 'He believed he had a vocation, and indeed I would say that the number of people at the service this morning proved him right.'

'Wouldn't there have been as many if he had not abandoned a medical career?'

'I don't know.' Sinclair sighed. 'Superintendent, as I told you, I have a date with the Le Merle family, so please ask whatever else you want to ask. I'll do my best to answer, and I'll treat our conversation as strictly confidential.'

'I apologize and I thank you.' Tansey was abashed. 'Did Father Le Merle ever tell you why he gave up medicine? His brother said he believed it was something to do with a girl who had died.'

'Yes, that's right. He talked about her quite a lot. Her name was Imogen, an unusual name, which I suppose is why I remember it.' Suddenly Sinclair laughed. 'But the story is nothing to Paul's discredit, if that's what you've been thinking, Superintendent. Rather the reverse. He offered to marry her.'

'Please tell me what you know, Father Sinclair,' Tansey said. 'It's possible, quite possible, that what happened all those years ago may have a connection with Father Le Merle's death,'

'Really? I can't imagine –' Sinclair frowned. 'Sorry I laughed. I'll certainly tell you what I know, but it isn't much and I doubt if it will help. However, here goes. Paul Le Merle went up to Oxford, aged nineteen, to read medicine. In his second year he met this girl called Imogen – I've no idea what her surname was, but it could have been Irish. She came from some remote part of Northern Ireland, and her parents were strict non-conformists. The trouble was that she became pregnant.'

'Did she tell her parents she was pregnant, but that Paul Le Merle had offered to marry her?'

'Good heavens, no. As she told Paul, her parents would have said they would rather have an illegitimate grandchild than a Roman Catholic son-in-law. But I digress –'

'I take it Paul *was* the man in question. You said "offered" to marry her, Father,' Tansey interrupted. 'I gathered from Christopher Le Merle that his brother had been deeply in love with this Imogen. A mere "offer" hardly sounds like blinding passion, does it?'

'Hardly, but Paul was not the man in question. He *was* deeply in love with her, that I'm sure of, though she didn't share his feelings. Imogen was in love with another man, the father of her child, who either couldn't or wouldn't marry her. She told Paul about her pregnancy because she needed money to pay for an abortion – they weren't so easy to arrange at that time, remember, and she was terrified her parents would learn of it – and Paul refused. He would give her money, but not for an abortion. It was contrary to his religious beliefs, and he felt very strongly about it. But the decision was to worry him for a long time.'

Sinclair paused, and Tansey, almost holding his breath as he anticipated the answer, said, 'The child's father couldn't afford an abortion. Did Father Le Merle know who he was?'

'Oh yes. He was a medico too, but not fully qualified. Anyway, he persuaded a friend, also a medical student, to help him perform the operation, quite illegally. Then something went wrong and Imogen died. Paul blamed himself for refusing her the money for a proper abortion, and of course he blamed the man. He said it was years before he came to terms with what had happened. Even after he had become a priest he found it difficult to forgive.'

'But what happened? There must have been scandal, or at least gossip – and they would surely have been sent down, their careers ruined.'

Sinclair nodded. 'I've no idea of the details, but in this case there was certainly no scandal. Somehow the whole affair was hushed up, and it was made to appear that it was all the girl's fault, that she had arranged a backstreet abortion for herself. The man got off scot-free.'

Tansey thought for a moment. 'I see,' he said slowly. 'So it's possible the chap that actually performed the operation with the help of his chum could still be practising?'

'It's possible,' Sinclair agreed. 'I don't know. Paul, Father Le Merle, hadn't mentioned the incident to me for a long time, but then there was no reason why he should have done, was there?'

'There might have been, if he had recently met the man again.' Tansey was getting a little impatient. 'Father Sinclair, you still haven't told me the man's name.'

'I've been trying to remember it,' Sinclair said mildly. 'It was an ordinary name, John or Joseph or Jack or James – something like that. I think it might have been John, but I couldn't swear to it. Not much help to you, I'm afraid.'

'And his last name? Any idea?'

'None, Superintendent. I don't believe I ever knew it. In retrospect, I'm not sure Paul didn't take care that I shouldn't know it, or Imogen's surname. He was always a kind man, and for the sake of the families he wouldn't want to start any rumours. But I could be imagining this.'

Tansey hid his disappointment. 'When did you last hear from Father Le Merle?' he asked.

'At Easter. I had a long letter from him,' Sinclair said. 'He sounded in fine form, and if he had come across someone from his past he never mentioned it.' He looked at his watch. 'Superintendent, I really –'

'Yes, I know, Father Sinclair.' Tansey got up off his chair. 'I'm going. Thank you very much for bearing with me. Have a good lunch, and please give my regards to Christopher Le Merle.'

'I will,' Sinclair promised.

But, in spite of the fact that he had hastened Tansey's departure, the priest didn't hurry immediately to his rendez-vous with the Le Merles. His heart was heavy. He had betrayed no trust, but he knew that he had given the super-intendent the motive he had been seeking for Father Le Merle's murder and, though he supposed it had been his duty, he was sure Paul Le Merle would not have approved. Paul would have said there was no reason to ruin a man's career and bring disgrace and misery to his family by resur-recting an old scandal – which had never been a scandal. But Paul, though no saint, had been a saintly man. The Whitelys were unlikely to feel so charitable towards the killer of their only child. And would the man, affected by some unsuspected fear, kill again?

Suddenly realizing that he was wasting time and achieving nothing, Father Sinclair locked up the church and set off for the Pomme d'Or. There was no point in regretting what he had told Tansey; in fact, he had had little choice. And now it was no longer up to him, but to the superintendent – and for that he was thankful.

Dick Tansey was not so thankful. It was true that at last a substantive motive for killing Father Le Merle had emerged; many people had killed to save their reputations, and with them their livelihoods. But it was hearsay: what Father Le Merle had once told Father Sinclair years ago. The rest was

166

circumstantial evidence, and most of this depended on the late Alfred Yorke. There was no genuine proof.

Tansey drove slowly back to Oxford, stopping on the way at a pub for a sandwich and half a pint of beer. He thought enviously of Sinclair and the Le Merles having lunch at the Pomme d'Or. But he had work to do.

He spent the best part of the afternoon in the public library. It was mostly frustrating research, but he learnt a few facts that were informative, if not necessarily of much importance. Knowing the year that Paul Le Merle had gone up to Oxford, he was able to pinpoint dates between which the tragedy to the girl must have occurred, and to ask to see microfilms of copies of the relevant *Oxford Mail*s. Nevertheless, to find what he was seeking proved a long and tiring task and he nearly abandoned it. Too often there were misleading headlines which raised his hopes, only to find them dashed as soon as he read the text. But perseverance paid off at last, and, when he had almost despaired, he found an item in the Stop Press column. After that it was simple.

Imogen Shaw had been twenty-one at the time of her death, and in her third year, reading history. She was said to be a good scholar and had been expected to get a First. She was described by various contemporaries, male and female, as 'attractive but shy', 'not really one of us', 'nice, pretty but difficult to get to know'. The impression Tansey received was that of a clever girl, a loner not sure of herself, who had been rather overwhelmed by Oxford after a strict, secluded childhood in an Irish village where her father had been the schoolmaster.

According to the *Oxford Mail*, she had not been without boyfriends, but none of them had been serious, none of them lasting. When she became pregnant, no one had come forward to admit responsibility or to offer help, and she had been forced to do what she could for herself. It was believed – it was not known for sure as she had never regained consciousness after being found by a fellow student in great pain, and taken to hospital – that she had procured a backstreet abortion, which had gone wrong. It was described as a 'A

Tragic Story' and published under a reproduction of the photograph that Father Le Merle had kept.

There was no mention of James Lancelot Ritchie, or of Paul Le Merle, who had both been up at the same college. But, while he was looking for further information on them, Tansey learnt that during that vital year Peter Quentin's father, Joseph Quentin, had also been a medical student, though a little older and more advanced than the other two, and that John Wessex had been on a special course in Oxford at the time.

'They're an ingrown lot, if ever there was one,' Tansey said to Whitelaw, whom, on his return to headquarters, he had been pleased to find in his office. 'It's all background, I suppose, but otherwise I haven't achieved much. We haven't a case against Ritchie. He only has to deny it.'

'But we can show our revered Chief Constable that he's been barking up the wrong tree,' Whitelaw said, trying not to sound triumphant. 'I've spent a large part of the day in Reading, where on the night Kathy Whitely was killed Alfred Yorke was in hospital. He gave a false name, but there's no doubt of the identification. He's been in and out of the hospital, I understand. They confirmed he had inoperable cancer and didn't have long to live, but there wasn't much they could do for him, and he kept discharging himself. So, unless we've got two killers, he's in the clear – apart from his attack on Ritchie, where anyway he came off worst.'

'Well, you've certainly been more successful than me.' Tansey was always generous. 'The trouble is that this business of Imogen Shaw was over thirty years ago, and then it was only a five-day wonder. I'm sure there must have been gossip, at least among the students, but gossip won't help much even if we could trace it. We need facts, proof.'

'What about Wessex or Quentin's pa? They should be worth a try. And there was obviously a cover-up.' Whitelaw was thoughtful. 'There might well be some old don around who would be prepared to tell what he knew.'

Tansey grinned, obviously pleased with himself. 'As a

matter of fact, I've already found a prospect. He lives alone in North Oxford, except for a housekeeper. He's over eighty and whether or not he'll talk I don't know, but he's agreed to see me tomorrow morning. Wish me luck.'

'I do indeed,' Whitelaw said fervently. 'We don't want the bugger to get away with another killing.'

Superintendent Tansey arrived punctually at 12.30 the next morning at the home of Professor Ian McFarling in North Oxford. It was a pleasant, unpretentious house with an air of well-being about it. A housekeeper in a neat black skirt and white blouse let Tansey in, and led him into a book-lined room where a tall, white-haired man rose to greet him.

'Good morning, Superintendent. I hope this time wasn't too inconvenient for you, but, as I said on the telephone yesterday, I always go to matins on Sunday mornings.'

'This is perfectly convenient, sir. It's very good of you to see me. I'll try not to keep you too long.'

The old man waved Tansey to a chair. 'I always have a glass or two of sherry at this time. I hope you will join me.'

'Thank you, sir.'

The sherry was poured and the two men seated themselves opposite each other. Professor McFarling regarded Tansey quizzically. 'Now, Superintendent, tell me what I can do for you. I'm curious, for I can't imagine why you should want to talk to me.'

'Sir, I'm investigating a case of murder – indeed a double murder – that of a priest and a young girl, a nurse, in Colombury. I assume you have read or heard something about it.'

'Yes, Superintendent, but my knowledge of the case is superficial, and that could be called an exaggeration.'

'Even though you knew Father Le Merle, Paul Le Merle?'

The old man's smile was thin. 'A long time ago, yes. I remember him as a pleasant young man, highly principled. I wasn't surprised when I heard he had become a priest. But

170

I've had no personal contact with him for years, not since he went down. We didn't part on very good terms.'

'Because you helped to cover up the true story of Imogen Shaw's death?' It was a blunt accusation. 'Sir, please tell me. No one is going to be prosecuted now for what happened then, but I need to know the facts.'

'Very well.' The old man sighed. 'In retrospect I'm not sorry for what I did, which was merely to keep silent. If I hadn't, they would both have been sent down, two promising careers ruined, two families made miserable and – what concerned me most – the college disgraced. And nothing would have brought the girl back.'

Tansey frowned. 'I don't understand. Why should Le Merle have been sent down? He'd done nothing wrong except to refuse to pay for an expensive London abortion – if that refusal was a sin. The baby wasn't his, and yet he offered to marry the girl.'

'I was not aware of that. But, as I said, he was a high-minded young man. I sometimes think that if he had had an atom of proof about the illegal operation, he would have blown the whole story – he didn't care about the reputation of the college – but he hadn't, so he walked out, went down from the university, to show his disdain.'

Tansey was beginning to dislike the old man; his own sympathies were with Le Merle. 'But you implied that two men were involved, sir?'

'You don't know who they were?'

'I know one, and I'll discover the name of the other, if necessary, though it would be simpler if you told me, sir – to prevent the need for inquiries which could cause gossip and publicity.'

There was a long silence, and Tansey wondered how the old man would react to the mild threat. But after a minute he rose, poured himself another sherry and lifted the bottle to Tansey in invitation. Tansey shook his head.

Then the professor said, 'All right, Superintendent, it's really a simple tale. The silly girl got pregnant, and because she was afraid of her parents she was determined on secrecy. James Ritchie, the father of the unborn, couldn't afford the kind of abortion she would have liked. She turned to Le Merle who, because of his principles, wouldn't help.

'Finally, Ritchie appealed to an old school friend, Joe Quentin, who was a couple of years ahead of him. The three of them, Ritchie, Quentin and the girl herself, agreed on self-help. Something went wrong, and she died. End of story, except that unluckily that evening the two men were seen by the righteous Le Merle helping the girl into a taxi and later, after she was dead and the results of the postmortem were known, he jumped to the right conclusions. He accused Ritchie. Ritchie denied everything. There was a fight, which brought me in as I had rooms underneath his and heard the racket and interrupted it. Anyway, under the system, Ritchie was responsible to me for his work and "general moral welfare", as it was called.'

'So you knew nothing about the operation until the incident was all over?'

'That's right, Superintendent. I didn't connive at it in advance.' The old man was cynical. 'My only sin was to protect the good name of the college and to take no action when a couple of days later Quentin and Ritchie confessed to me what they had done. And that's all I can tell you.' Clearly he did not want to be involved.

'Just one more question, sir. Why did Quentin allow himself to be involved?'

'I don't really know. They were old friends. Ritchie couldn't have done it by himself, and it was convenient that Quentin was living in digs, not in college.' The retired professor stood up. 'Now, Superintendent, I'm sorry, but it's time for my lunch.'

'Of course, sir,' Tansey said. 'I won't keep you. Thank you very much for being so patient and so frank. I trust I shan't have to bother you again.'

And let him think about that last remark of mine, Tansey said to himself vindictively as he drove away from Professor McFarling's house. I hope it gives him a few bad dreams, damn him. He never expressed even conventional regret at Father Le Merle's death or at the grief that the Le Merle family has been caused. Tansey guessed that whatever the young Paul Le Merle had said to the professor at their last meeting had rankled badly.

On Monday morning, after a brief conference, Superintendent Tansey and Inspector Whitelaw agreed to divide their labours. Whitelaw would get Dr Joseph Quentin's address and, unless he lived too far away, would interview him, while Tansey would go to Colombury and talk to Ritchie. They agreed that old Professor McFarling might have warned his former students, but Tansey thought this unlikely – the old man had struck him as completely self-centred – and the superintendent hoped that the element of surprise in the interrogations of Ritchie and Quentin might yield further information, and conceivably a confession, though the last seemed highly improbable.

Driving down to Tunbridge Wells on the Kent–Sussex border on a fine autumnal day, Whitelaw concluded that he had the best of the deal. There had been no difficulty in obtaining Dr Joseph Quentin's address. Bernard Cross had it on record as the home of Dr Peter Quentin, and Cross asked no questions. By now he was getting used to strange requests from the police, and he was preoccupied with arrangements for Alfred Yorke's funeral, which was expected to take place the following week, and for which Angela Cross was determined to be responsible. Whitelaw grinned to himself as he recalled Cross's exasperation at the unwanted task imposed upon him, and thought that he would be better pleased when he read that day's *Courier*, and learnt that the police no longer suspected Alfred Yorke of killing either Father Le Merle or Nurse Whitely.

It was a reasonably long drive from Oxford, but the bulk of the traffic was travelling in the other direction, and Whitelaw enjoyed driving. His only problem was where to park when he reached his destination, but, this solved, he walked to Dr Quentin's surgery, obeying the notice on the front door and following an arrow to a side door, which he entered, again according to instructions, without ringing the bell.

The surgery was on the ground floor of a substantial house, which was clearly also the family home. He found himself in a waiting room full of patients, or so it seemed to him, mostly women with small children. A girl in a white coat, sitting behind a desk, regarded him suspiciously.

'Please come here. I need your name. You're a registered patient of Dr Quentin?' she asked.

'No, I am not. My name is Whitelaw. Inspector Whitelaw and –'

'All right, Mr Whitelaw. Sit down there, please. You will be called in due course.'

'Inspector Whitelaw,' he corrected her, and showed her his warrant card.

She shrugged. 'You'll still have to take your turn, Inspector.'

Whitelaw took a slim notebook from his pocket, wrote, 'Inspector Whitelaw, Thames Valley Police, to see Dr Quentin about Imogen Shaw *now*'. He tore off the page and folded it. 'Please give this to Dr Quentin at once.' It was an order.

The girl glared at him, but she took the message. Whitelaw waited by her desk. Two minutes later she was back, escorting an old woman who was walking with difficulty. 'You may go in, Inspector,' she said stiffly.

The doctor rose as Whitelaw came into his office, but he didn't offer his hand. 'Good morning, Inspector. I've been expecting a visit from you or your equivalent.'

'You have, Doctor? Why?'

'I reckoned there might be trouble once I learned that Mr Ritchie and Father Le Merle had met again and then that Le Merle had been killed. I thought the police might delve into the past, however irrelevant it might prove.'

'I see. Why do you believe that the past is irrelevant in this case, Dr Quentin?'

Quentin raised his eyebrows. 'Surely, Inspector, you've got your man – that poor old vagrant who attacked Ritchie. There's no question, is there? After all, as I understand it, there were reputable witnesses to his attack on poor Ritchie.'

'There were indeed, Dr Quentin, but it is most improbable that Yorke killed Father Le Merle, and he certainly did not kill Nurse Whitely. He has a cast-iron alibi for the nurse's murder, and we think she was only killed because she had been in St Stephen's church at the vital time, and might have knowledge of the killer. Yorke had no motive for killing either Le Merle or Whitely, Dr Quentin. I repeat, no credible motive.'

'Are you suggesting that *I* had a motive?' Dr Quentin said suddenly. 'Inspector, if it became generally known that as a young man I had performed an operation illegally on Imogen Shaw – which I gather is what you're threatening – I would probably lose a few patients. They wouldn't like the idea of their GP committing such an unpleasant act. But I doubt if I would be struck off after all these years, or that it would mean more to me than a certain amount of unwanted publicity, and some dirt on the good name of Quentin. Would you really say that this gives me a motive for murder?'

'Frankly, no, Doctor.'

'Good – and incidentally, the first Saturday of the month when Father Le Merle was killed, I was at home all the weekend with my wife *and* her parents.'

He's getting rattled, Whitelaw thought, and said, 'You and Mr Ritchie are close friends.'

'We're friends, yes. We go a long way back, to our school days, in fact. And, as you probably know, he's been very kind and helpful to my son, Peter, who, unlike me, is ambitious, and is planning to follow the same kind of career as Ritchie.'

'Not starting with a botched abortion, I assume. Is your son aware of this, er, incident in your mutual pasts, Doctor?'

Quentin gritted his teeth. 'Yes. I warned him. I had to consider his future. He hopes to get into one of the big London teaching hospitals, and I had to advise him not to offer Ritchie's name as a sponsor, in case – '

'In case there's a scandal.' Whitelaw finished the sentence for him. 'Mr Ritchie, of course, as a consultant gynaecologist, is far more vulnerable than you are, and I appreciate that it would do no good for your son to be closely associated with him.'

Quentin stood up and started pacing up and down the office. 'There is no reason, no reason whatsoever, why there should be a scandal unless you police create one – sell the story to the media, perhaps; isn't that what policemen do nowadays? What happened in Oxford years ago is past history, it has nothing to do with Le Merle's death. How could it? I didn't kill him. Ritchie didn't kill him.'

'Are you sure?'

Quentin stopped pacing. For a moment he said nothing. Then he shouted, 'Get out! Get out of my office! Out of my house!' He lifted his hand, his fist clenched, as if he were about to strike Whitelaw, but fortunately he thought better of it. He jabbed at the bellpush on his desk and when the white-coated girl answered it, which she did with astonishing promptitude, he said with a fairly restrained voice, 'The inspector is leaving. Show him out.'

'Thank you,' Whitelaw said, taking his time over his departure. 'Thank you very much, Dr Quentin. You've been most helpful, given both of us food for thought, no doubt. Good morning to you.'

While Inspector Whitelaw was antagonizing Dr Joseph Quentin, Superintendent Tansey had reached Colombury and, having assured himself that Lance Ritchie was making excellent progress and would be out of the hospital in a couple of days, had gone along to Ritchie's room. The doctor was sitting up in bed, reading the *Courier*, and indeed looked much better. He greeted Tansey with civility, if not with pleasure.

'More questions, Superintendent? Don't you ever run out of them?'

'Not as a rule, at least not until a case is closed, sir.'

'Ah well, I've been doing some thinking and I've come to the conclusion that Yorke attacked me because he believed I had killed Le Merle. Is that conceivable? According to today's *Courier*, the police no longer suspect Yorke himself.'

'That is so, sir. Yorke is in the clear.'

'But why did he pick on me?'

'For the same reason that Nurse Whitely did – your aftershave lotion, which has a very strong smell of musk. They both smelt you as you passed them in St Stephen's church on the evening of Father Le Merle's murder. Kathy Whitely

176

subsequently recognized the scent when she fainted and you tried to help her up. Yorke recognized it when you seized him in the hospital grounds as he was running away from Dr Quentin. Incidentally, Mr Ritchie, what were you doing in the church that evening? Or do you deny you were there?'

Lance Ritchie drew a deep breath, which must have hurt him for he winced. 'What the hell!' he said. 'No, I don't deny it. I should have told you before, Superintendent, but it would have meant explanations. I needed to see Paul Le Merle. I had been putting it off, but that evening I decided I had to act. I tried the presbytery first. There was no answer, so I went into the church. It was in darkness, but there was a light shining around the door which I assumed led to the sacristy. You see, Le Merle knew something about my past which could ruin me and do a . . . a friend no good if it became public property. Father Le Merle had no positive proof, but if the media got hold of the story, it would be enough. I had to know what Paul intended to do. The uncertainty was driving me up the wall.'

'You're referring to the operation that you and Dr Joseph Quentin performed illegally on Imogen Shaw?' Tansey said, when Ritchie found it difficult to proceed. 'Professor McFarling has told us about the, er, incident.'

'Has he indeed? You've been busy, Superintendent.' Ritchie was bitter. 'Yes, the professor kept his mouth shut at the time, for the sake of the college, he said, but he's not minded about the good name of the college so much since he was forced to resign after being accused of publishing the work of one of his pupils as his own. But I've got no excuse for what I did. I couldn't afford to marry Imogen, which was what she really wanted, and anyway I had no desire to saddle myself with a wife and child at that stage of my career. Abortion seemed the answer, but she was paranoid about secrecy because of her family – and then things went wrong.'

Dick Tansey, who had previously rather disliked Ritchie, felt a sudden rush of sympathy for him. But he reminded himself that the killing of Father Le Merle had been premeditated and the priest, a good man, much loved, had not deserved such a death. Glancing at Ritchie, he was surprised to see that he was smiling, albeit wanly.

'Now I shall never know what Le Merle proposed to do, whether he was going to take his revenge – he had been desperately in love with Imogen – and do his best to make my name and Joe Quentin's stink, or whether because of the passing of time and his religious vocation he was able to forgive.' Ritchie shook his head sadly. 'It makes no difference now, but I would like to have known.'

'You didn't ask him, then? Why not, if it was so important to you?'

'Ask him? How could I?' Ritchie sounded disbelieving. 'Superintendent, I didn't kill Paul Le Merle. He was already dead when I went into the sacristy. But he'd not been dead long. I felt for a pulse, to be sure. The body was still warm. In fact, I could easily have met his killer as I came into the church.' He stopped. 'You don't believe me, do you?'

Tansey met his gaze, which was steady. 'I really don't know, Mr Ritchie. At the moment I'm keeping an open mind,' he said.

CHAPTER 20

'Means,' Superintendent Tansey said. 'A sharp knife, available in any department store and therefore able to be bought anonymously. The ability to use it is not so easy to come by, though. Remember the difficulty Yorke had trying to knife Ritchie.'

Inspector Whitelaw nodded. 'Ghent made the point that it was either medical skill or luck that allowed one blow to kill Le Merle. But would the killer have accepted luck, and departed without striking again? It would seem to me unlikely. In my opinion he knew he had been successful because he had medical know-how.'

It was the afternoon of the same day and the two men, having spent some time going through the files and verifying certain points, were now reviewing the case. They were clear in their own minds about who had killed Father Le Merle and subsequently Nurse Whitely, but they were still seeking final confirmation.

'Opportunity,' Tansey said. 'He had the opportunity. We know he was around that part of the town at the approximate time, and he was in a position to have learned of Father Le Merle's habits.'

'According to your report, Ritchie said that he went first to the presbytery. That's interesting, isn't it?' Whitelaw said.

'Yes,' Tansey agreed. 'And I'd swear it wasn't a lie. He volunteered the information quite naturally. Ritchie's not been very long in Colombury, and he's not a Catholic. He did what was obvious, what you or I might have done if we'd been looking for the priest.'

'The behaviour of an innocent man, in fact?' It was scarcely a question.

'That's right,' Tansey affirmed. 'So, let's continue. Lastly we come to motive: to prevent Le Merle publishing the story of the illegal operation on Imogen Shaw. I consulted Ghent about the consequences if it did become public. He wasn't sure about the legal position, but he believes the BMA would take no action, because neither Ritchie not Quentin were qualified doctors at the time, only students. However, that doesn't mean that the results for them would be pleasant if the media got hold of the story. Ghent thinks Ritchie would be politely asked to resign and would have difficulty in finding another hospital, and Quentin would lose a lot of his patients. And he pointed out, as if we didn't know, that any such scandal would affect those closely associated with them – especially any who happened to be connected with the medical profession.'

'Yes. Means, opportunity, motive are all fine for the murder of Father Le Merle,' Whitelaw said, 'but what worries me is that although the means, showing medical know-how, and the opportunity apply to Kathy Whitely's murder, the motive does not. It's a *non sequitur*. Why should he have killed Whitely? Wouldn't it have been more sensible to have merely ignored her?'

'The point's worried me too,' Tansey admitted. 'But I've come up with an explanation. We're dealing with a devious character, remember. I think he discovered she had been the nurse in St Stephen's that the *Courier* publicized so much – as indeed we did also. It didn't bother him because he knew she had nothing on him, but he realized that everyone – media and police – believed she might be able to point to the killer and, from what she said to her boyfriend, Brian Minton, she believed this herself.' Tansey paused, and then continued.

'To kill her would, therefore, encourage this belief, and give the murderer a kind of alibi because, when he left her that Saturday night, he went straight to the Windrush Arms as he told us he had. We checked and Mrs Burke remembered him making a joke about poor bachelors having to do their own shopping; he was carrying a plastic bag, probably containing the chalice and a pair of surgical gloves, but at the time this meant nothing to us. What do you think?'

'It's certainly ingenious,' Whitelaw said. 'And if we accept it, I'd say we have a case.'

'Good,' said Tansey. 'Let's go and talk to Dr Peter Quentin.'

They were leaving the office when Tansey's secretary called the reception desk to tell him that Mr Cross was on the phone and wished to speak to the superintendent urgently. Reluctantly they returned.

'Yes, Mr Cross. Tansey here. What's the trouble?' He listened for a moment and said, 'What?' and, covering the mouthpiece, added to Whitelaw: 'Ritchie's tried to commit suicide.'

'Dear God!' Whitelaw muttered.

'What happened?' Tansey asked Cross.

'He was meant to be resting after lunch,' Cross said. 'As you know, he's no longer in intensive care and no one was watching him. He must have gone along to Sister's room and, when she wasn't there, taken a bottle of sedatives from her drugs cupboard.'

'Wasn't it locked?'

'He has a key. Luckily one of the nurses looked in on him, thought he was making funny noises, saw the bottle and a note beside his bed, and called for help.'

'How is he? Will he live?'

'He's having his stomach pumped out right now,' Cross said. 'As for living, I don't know. He's a strong man physically, but it's only a day or two since he was attacked and had a major operation. We'll have to wait and see.'

'You mentioned a note,' Tansey prompted when Cross, in his distress, fell silent.

'Yes, it was addressed to me. It said, "Sorry. I've never killed anyone intentionally, but I can't go on. Tansey will explain." And that's what I want, Superintendent, an explanation, dammit.' Cross was suddenly angry.

'Of course,' Tansey said soothingly. 'And you shall have an explanation, Mr Cross. Inspector Whitelaw and I were about to start for Colombury when your call came through. We have business there which may take us a while, but as

181

soon as possible we'll come to the hospital. Will you wait?'

'Yes, I'm waiting to know about Ritchie anyway. If he dies –'

'Let us hope he doesn't, Mr Cross. We'll see you shortly. Goodbye.'

Tansey put down the receiver and heaved a sigh. He looked at Whitelaw. 'You gathered the gist? I'll fill you in as we go. This is a complication we could have done without.'

Dr Peter Quentin did not make the two detective officers welcome. 'What the hell do you want now?' he demanded when his landlady announced them. 'I'm working.' He gestured to the table at the end of the room laden with books and papers, where he had been sitting, and Whitelaw noted the half-empty glass of what looked like whisky nestling among the confusion.

Tansey didn't apologize. 'Surely your father warned you that we might be calling,' he said.

'What if he did?' Quentin demanded aggressively. 'I can't be available twenty-four hours a day to answer your questions.'

'Dr Quentin, we're investigating two murders, two deliberate killings, and we believe you can help us with our inquiries.'

'You mean that, having failed through some abysmal stupidity to pin the crimes on that sod, Alfred Yorke, you're trying to pin them on Lance Ritchie because of something that happened before I was born?'

Tansey didn't dispute the accusation. He said, 'When did your father tell you about this "something that happened before you were born", Dr Quentin?'

'When I was at home one weekend some while ago. Does it matter?'

'Before Father Le Merle was killed?'

Quentin shrugged. 'I'd have to look it up,' he said.

'You keep a diary?' Tansey said, thinking that Quentin was a cool customer though he seemed very tense. 'May I see?'

'It's more of an engagement book than a diary,' said Quentin, but he didn't object to showing it to Tansey.

182

As the doctor stood up to pass the book to the superintendent, Whitelaw noticed that he staggered slightly. While Tansey leafed through the pages, the inspector wandered over to the table with its litter of books and papers. There was, he saw, a bottle of whisky, a good third empty, half-hidden behind a thick table leg. Peter Quentin might have been working before they interrupted him, but he had also been drinking.

'Fine,' Tansey said, handing back the book. 'It seems you learnt of the operation which Mr Ritchie and your father performed illegally when they were students, the weekend before Father Le Merle was killed.'

'So what?'

'And the Sunday of that weekend you drove out to Chipping Norton to visit friends. You would have driven past the house of Mr and Mrs Pettigrew.'

'I don't know the Pettigrews.'

'No,' Tansey said. He didn't explain that the chalice stolen from St Stephen's church had been found in the Pettigrews' garden; Quentin would have learnt that from the *Courier*.

The phone rang and Quentin leapt to answer, but only to be disappointed. 'No,' he said. 'I'm busy. I can't talk now. I'll call you tomorrow.'

'You're expecting a phone call, Doctor?' Tansey asked as Quentin returned to his seat.

'Yes, I am,' he said after a brief hesitation. Then anger overcame caution, 'From the hospital, to learn whether you've succeeded in hounding Lance Ritchie to his death.'

'So you've heard he's in a bad way?' Tansey said.

'Yes, and all thanks to you. Why the hell you've had to rake up an ancient wrong-doing and try to turn it into a major scandal, I can't imagine.'

'I'll tell you why.' Tansey was curt. 'Father Le Merle was killed because his killer was afraid he would publicize this "ancient wrong-doing", as you call it. He was afraid it would bring disgrace to his name and, if not ruin his career, at least by association do it no good.'

'Okay, Superintendent,' said Quentin. 'You've found a possible motive for Mr Ritchie. As to means, he could easily have bought a knife to stick in Le Merle, and he'd know how to chop down with the side of his hand on Kathy Whitely's spinal cord, or if that didn't go quite right to pull her into the bushes and strangle her. Agreed?'

'Agreed,' Tansey said calmly.

Neither Superintendent Tansey nor Inspector Whitelaw had betrayed by the widening of an eye or a caught breath that Peter Quentin had just condemned himself. There had been no mention in any of the media that Nurse Whitely's killer had strangled her because his first attack on her had not been completely successful. Dr Ghent had promised that this information should be a carefully guarded secret, and it had been well kept.

'That leaves opportunity, then,' Peter Quentin continued. 'Superintendent, Mr Ritchie was at a party given in his honour by the Crosses that Saturday evening. Are you seriously telling me that he killed Father Le Merle and then went out to supper?'

'No, Dr Quentin, I'm not telling you that,' Tansey said. 'That's your scenario, not mine. Actually Mr Ritchie was in St Stephen's church at about 5.30 that evening, as he has admitted.'

'He's admitted it?' Quentin was genuinely surprised. 'But – Superintendent Tansey, are you now suggesting that Mr Ritchie has admitted to killing Father Le Merle?'

Tansey didn't answer the question. He said, 'Nurse Whitely had left you by then, Dr Quentin, and gone into the church, and you were off to the Windrush Arms. Meg Burke remembers you on that evening, joking about your shopping bag.'

'I don't understand what you're getting at, Superintendent.' Quentin had become uneasy.

'It doesn't matter,' Tansey said. 'I digressed. We were discussing the case against Mr Ritchie. It seems he had means, opportunity and motive. A pity that an attempt to hide a sordid little story which almost certainly Father Le Merle had no intention of publicizing ended in two killings – which would exaggerate the importance of the whole affair enormously.'

'But that's absurd. You can't –'

Tansey ignored the interruption. 'Mr Ritchie has been very good to you, hasn't he, Dr Quentin? Helped to further your career, always ready to offer you support, say a word in the right place – in fact, a friend at court. Ironic this should have happened.' Tansey was on his feet, nodding to Whitelaw that they were about to leave. 'We'll say good evening then, Doctor. We won't keep you from your work any longer.'

'You've got it wrong!' Quentin exclaimed.

'Oh no, we have not, Doctor.' Tansey shook his head. 'We were merely creating a possible scenario. We know that Mr Ritchie killed neither Father Le Merle nor Kathy Whitely. The priest was already dead when Mr Ritchie found him and before Nurse Whitely went into the church. He had been killed some ten or fifteen minutes earlier than we had at first thought. But you knew this, didn't you, Doctor?'

'That was as good as an accusation,' Whitelaw said as the two men walked to the hospital. 'And you hadn't given him any official warning.'

'Too bad,' Tansey said. 'We'll have him in tomorrow and give him the works. I think he'll break, and with luck we'll be able to avoid too many bits of loose change.'

'You mean, limit the damage?'

Tansey nodded, and Whitelaw wondered if he would ever understand this officer, who was always prepared to antagonize his superiors, to go out of his way to bend the law, to risk any promotion, not only in order to bring the guilty to justice, but also to protect those involved by reason of mischance or even their own foolishness.

They reached the hospital and went straight to Cross's office, where Bernard Cross and Brigadier Wessex were deep in worried conversation. Tansey at once asked after Ritchie.

'At least that's one piece of good news,' Cross said. 'He's going to be fine, Superintendent, but he's much too weak to talk at the moment. And we want to know why he tried to take his own life. You promised an explanation.'

Tansey looked doubtfully at Wessex. Ritchie had left a note for Cross, who was indeed owed an explanation, but that did not include the brigadier.

As if reading his thoughts, Cross said, 'Brigadier Wessex is a

185

governor of the hospital and is completely in my confidence, Superintendent. I've already told him all I know about Lance Ritchie, and the note he left me.'

Tansey thought, the brigadier may be completely in your confidence, but he's not in mine. However, he saw no point in making a fuss. 'Right,' he said. 'I'll explain as well as I can, but I'm only a policeman. You both know more about the medical world than I do. Incidentally, I'm sure you both realize that all this is absolutely confidential.'

'Get on with it,' Wessex said gruffly.

The superintendent got on with it. The inspector added the odd remark. There was only one interruption. The name of Imogen Shaw meant nothing to Wessex, but he recalled the incident of the girl dying after a botched abortion.

'There was a lot of talk at the university,' he said. 'At that time I was there on a course and I remember the arguments about the rights of women over their own bodies, and whether or not there should be free condoms in all JCRs. But I didn't know either Ritchie or Quentin then, and I never even heard a whisper that students were responsible for the girl's death.'

Tansey continued, asking when he had finished his account of the case, 'How will this affect Mr Ritchie's standing at the hospital? Will he lose his job if there's a scandal, even though the affair is now past history?'

Cross shrugged. 'Does it matter? If you're going to accuse him of murder, Superintendent –'

'But we're not, Mr Cross. Mr Ritchie didn't kill either Father Le Merle or Nurse Whitely, I assure you.'

'Thank God for that!' Cross said. 'I can't say he's the easiest man to get on with, but he's a fine doctor and –'

'If he didn't kill them, who did?' Wessex demanded. 'And why was Father Le Merle killed if it wasn't for fear that this old story would resurface? What's more, it was a baseless fear. Father Le Merle was the best of men and would never have ruined, or tried to ruin anyone, whatever he might have done.'

But Tansey and Whitelaw were already on their feet. 'I'm afraid we're not at liberty to tell you any more at present,'

Tansey said, 'except that we hope to make an arrest very soon. Please dismiss Mr Ritchie's suicide attempt as the result of depression after Yorke's attack on him and his operation, and reassure him that he's under no suspicion for the killings.'

The two men objected, Wessex the more vociferously, but the superintendent was adamant. They would have to wait and see.

No one had long to wait. In the small hours of the next day Dr Peter Quentin took his own life, and in so doing he was far more efficient than Lance Ritchie, perhaps because he knew that he was guilty and there would be no escape from the consequences. He gave himself an intravenous injection of an overdose of morphia, which he had stolen from the hospital in case he should need it. He died, presumably peacefully, in his sleep.

Before he died, however, he wrote and signed a confession. He admitted to killing Father Le Merle and Kathy Whitely. He said that he had killed Le Merle because he had told the priest, in a moment of confidence, that he had caused the death of a married woman who was his mistress by attempting to abort their child, and he was afraid that Le Merle might make this public, and thus ruin his career. He said that he had killed Kathy Whitely when he realized that her death would imply that Le Merle had been killed ten or fifteen minutes after it had actually happened, and so give him an alibi. He did not express regret for what he had done, but he did express the hope that this full confession would put the record straight and put an end to all supposition and rumour.

'What do you make of it?' Whitelaw asked Tansey as soon as he had read it.

'The same as you, I would guess,' Tansey said. 'Half truth, half lies. Quentin knew he hadn't a hope himself, but he wanted to save his father and Ritchie from the results of a scandal.'

'So he invented the married mistress?'

'Why not? He had nothing to lose.'

187

'We accept her?'

'Certainly, though we don't waste the taxpayer's money looking for her. If the media want to chase her, let them. We'll leave it alone. This way the least damage is done to Ritchie, to Joe Quentin and to the hospital.'

Whitelaw laughed. 'So all's well that ends well,' he said cynically, and thought that if the Thames Valley Police Serious Crime Squad didn't get much credit, it was too bad; no one should be as ambitious as Peter Quentin had proved unless they were made of sterner stuff.